CENTURY

CENTURY

Sarah Singleton

SIMON AND SCHUSTER

For my grandmother Sybil, with love

SIMON AND SCHUSTER

First published in Great Britain in 2005 by Simon & Schuster UK Ltd
A Viacom company

Simon & Schuster UK Ltd
Africa House, 64-78 Kingsway
London WC2B 6AH

A CIP catalogue record for this book is available from the British Library

ISBN 1 416 90135 3

1 3 5 7 9 10 8 6 4 2

Printed and bound in Great Britain by Cox & Wyman, Reading, Berkshire

www.simonsays.co.uk

Prologue

The book lay hidden in a wooden crate in the attic over the west wing of the house. The place was undergoing renovation, after decades of standing empty. A few rotten pieces of furniture remained, but the residents were long gone. The old roof tiles had slipped and needed renewing. From the roofspace workmen carried down chests of mouldering rags, tin boxes full of papers, old lampshades, mounds of velvet curtains. Covered in dust, the forgotten things huddled in the great hall. Most would end up at the tip.

An expert prodded the junk, hoping for a valuable find. An oil painting, perhaps. An antique gown free from the ravages of moth larvae and mould. A vase, a collection of jewellery. But he couldn't find anything. Even the papers were dull – faded housekeeping receipts detailing pounds, shillings and pence paid for grocery deliveries.

He opened the wooden crate. It was busy with spiders, and puffed a breath of sour dust.

The expert tugged out the remains of children's clothes, chewed into a mouse's nest.

"Nothing," he said. "Worthless." Then, delving deeper, he found something. "Just a minute," he said, coughing. "What's this?"

He pulled out a book. A cover of faded red leather, worn at the edges. A thick piece of string bound the book like a parcel, knotted and knotted again.

The expert took a penknife from his pocket and cut the string. He opened the book and turned the pages, peering down his nose. He read, briefly, then shut the book with a snap.

"It's a novel," he said. "Some kind of romance. Little value, but maybe you'll find the story of interest. The author's name is written in the front. Here, have a look."

He handed the book to me.

Century

A Novel

by Mercy Galliena Verga

1890

I

A woman under the ice.

A ghost. Mercy could see ghosts, the echoes of people who had died. The dead moved on to another world, to heaven perhaps, or Valhalla if you were a Viking. Sometimes they left threads of themselves behind, like a piece of cloth snagged from a dress, or strands of hair caught on a nail. Only, of course, the ghosts were immaterial, and the snags were places people held onto, where something important had happened. Perhaps, Mercy wondered, you did not even have to be dead to leave a ghost. Perhaps she had already left some of her own.

The woman under the ice. The pond was a black pocket at the end of Distillery Meadow, with trees hunched over. It was the hour before dawn and the sky had paled in the east. Frosty fields spread away.

Mercy was tired. She was a thin, sullen-looking girl with a closed face, given to long hours of brooding. She had thick black hair and a dark coat. She had walked right across the meadow. Now her legs felt heavy and stiff, and her head ached. It was the end of night – and also, the end of her day. The Verga family always awoke just after sunset, and retired to bed before dawn.

She was sitting on the cold bank by the pond and she prodded the ice with her booted foot. It felt thick. Then she saw her, the ghost woman, face up, in a blur, her hair a dark stream, and her dress a white, watery billow. The woman flowed.

When the ghost's face was under Mercy's feet, her eyes opened – blank holes which reflected the violet in the sky. The ice, imperfectly clear, veiled her features.

Mercy gasped, though she knew the ghost for what it was. The other ghosts – she had seen them so many times. They were familiar, unnoticed, like the old paintings on the wall. Not this one. Mercy wasn't afraid, but the sight was still a shock – this new face. Like jumping into cold water, or tripping over. Her skin seemed to prickle, from the base of her spine to the top of her head.

She stood up and backed away from the pond, but she couldn't tear her eyes from the ghost. The woman's hair undulated in gentle currents. She opened her mouth, and closed it again, like a fish. Perhaps she was trying to say something. Mercy did not wait to find out. She gathered up her skirts and ran across Distillery Meadow. She didn't stop until she reached the house.

The house was called Century. It reared above a ha-ha,

which was a ditch and wall to keep the cattle from the garden. The house overlooked parkland, the meadows and, further away, a huge lake, like a ribbon of mercury.

Mercy ran up the steps to the garden, through the gateway in the high wall around the rose garden and pushed through the door into the kitchens, where Aurelia was stooped over, stoking the fire. Hearing the door bang, she turned round.

"Mercy!" she scolded. "Why are you always so noisy?"

Aurelia was thin, in a tight black dress, with white hair pinned in a bun. When she realised how shocked and breathless Mercy was, her expression changed from annoyance to concern.

"Mercy," she said again, more gently now. "What happened? Mercy my dear, sit down. You're cold – your face is quite blue! Look at your hands – your arms. The blood has stopped in your fingers. Sit down by the fire."

She ushered Mercy to the little wooden chair by the fire, unlaced Mercy's boots, and rubbed her feet to warm them. Mercy recovered her breath and tried to speak but her lips and tongue were too cold. Aurelia warmed milk, and poured it in a cup with cinnamon, for Mercy to drink. Slowly, Mercy recovered. Her hands throbbed and tingled as they warmed.

"Now, what happened?" Aurelia said, patiently rubbing the soles of Mercy's tiny feet.

"I saw a new one," Mercy said. "I saw a ghost. Under the ice in the little pond at the end of Distillery Meadow."

Aurelia sat up straight. "Why did you do that? Why did you go to the meadow?"

7

Aurelia was alarmed, because Century's days were endless and unchanging. Nothing new or strange should ever happen. Maybe even the suggestions of dawn and dusk were an illusion and the house was eternally cloaked in darkness.

But Aurelia knew what Mercy could see, and she believed her. At first, when Mercy had told them about the ghosts, everyone had assumed she was making it up. Lots of children have invisible friends. Mercy's invisible friends did not fade away and in any case such talents were not unusual in the family. Trajan, her father, had long ago told Mercy that his maternal great-aunt had also seen ghosts, and everyone came to accept it. Every day, Mercy saw the ghost of a ginger cat in the kitchen. It jumped to the top of the dresser, curled up and fell asleep. Sometimes she could see a man in a gardener's uniform picking apples in the orchard. Like wallpaper, most of them; faded into the background, unremarkable.

Aurelia, housekeeper and nurse, did not like this seeing of ghosts. She pursed her lips and shook her head. Indeed, Mercy thought, she acted as though it were a bad habit, like biting fingernails or whistling, which Mercy should have the firmness of character to give up. As if she could!

"Were you afraid?" Aurelia asked.

"Not afraid, exactly. It's like – having a cold fish dropped down your back. Or suddenly sneezing. A shock!"

"Hmmph," Aurelia said. "You shouldn't be out so close to morning. You never go to the meadow! What were you

8

thinking of? You haven't the strength to walk so far. Why didn't you stay in the garden? Perhaps your mind was playing tricks."

Mercy frowned. She knew what she had seen. And what had prompted her to take a different walk? After all, it wasn't something she'd done for a long time. For months? How long had it been? It was hard to tell. One day was so much like another in the big house. She rose after sunset, for the long midwinter night. She ate breakfast with her younger sister Charity, and then took their lessons with the governess. After lunch the girls helped in the kitchen, and Mercy took a walk in the garden. It was a moment of pleasure, her usual stroll through the bare rose bushes, beneath the stars.

Today though – something extraordinary. Curious dreams in the night and, on waking, a snowdrop upon her pillow. The crisp, white, vital flower, just inches from her face. Where had it come from? Nothing grew in the gardens and grounds of Century. The earth was frozen, hard as iron. She had picked up the flower from the pillow and marvelled, touching the tender white petals with her fingertips, trying to breathe any faint perfume it might possess. The snowdrop was a mystery. The sight was a jolt.

She had thought about the flower all the long, dark day; keeping it secret and brooding over its origin. Had Charity, Aurelia or her father placed it there, beside her sleeping head, as a surprise? She waited for the culprit to reveal himself.

Then, when she took her usual walk in the garden, she had

remembered that snowdrops used to grow by the pond in Distillery Meadow, so she had turned on her heels and headed off. She had broken the usual pattern.

Mercy couldn't remember the last time she'd seen the little pond. So long, long ago, in the spring that never returned, when the pond was a cool green jewel, floating with the ghostly jelly of frogspawn. But the flower reminded her of Januarys past, when the pond was skirted with crowds of snowdrops. Harbingers of spring in the darkest days. Had the flowers bloomed again? She hadn't found any snowdrops but she now knew the pond held a secret of its own.

Odd thoughts scratched inside her head, like a dream she couldn't catch. She rubbed at her hair. Her feet itched. Aurelia was staring at her.

"Go to bed now," she said. "You look tired."

In Mercy's bedroom a fire burned in the small iron hearth, bordered with blue and white tiles. Aurelia helped Mercy undress and tied the ribbons on her white nightgown, brushed Mercy's long black hair and hung up her faded silk dress.

Mercy jumped into bed, pulling up the covers. "Aurelia, how long have we lived here?" she asked.

"Goodness gracious, I can't remember." Aurelia bustled, drawing the dusty curtains, folding Mercy's shawl.

"Well, about how long?"

"We moved to Century from Italy," Aurelia said quickly. "From Rome. The old country."

"I know. How long ago?"

10

"A long time. I don't know." Aurelia stood up straight, frowning. "A long time," she said. "Go to sleep."

But Mercy lay awake awhile, conscious of her heart beating against her ribs. She stretched her arms and legs. The ghost drifted in her mind, in the white cloud of her dress. How long had the winter lasted? She hadn't thought to ask before. The endless winter nights stretched behind, in a kind of waking dream. And she had moved through them like a sleep-walker. Something had prompted her to seek out the forgotten pond. The pattern of days was broken.

Mercy woke in the evening. Unusually, she drew the curtains. The moon curved like a silver saucer over the trees. She pulled off her nightgown. A bruise flowered on her knee where she had fallen, petals of mauve and red on white skin. She was very thin, with arms like ivory sticks, but her hair was a rich black, and long, right down to her waist. A robe to hide in.

She pulled on her underclothes, fastened the corset and the pink dress. The soft silk wrinkled, like old rose petals.

Charity was sitting at the table in the old nursery parlour. She toyed with a tarnished silver egg-cup. Three soft white-bread soldiers lay upon a plate painted with blue roses. She dipped one soldier in the yolk, and bit off its head. Then she put the bread down.

"Is that all you can eat?" Mercy said. She sat at the other end of the table. Most of the great house had been abandoned to the dust and mice, but here flames crackled on cedar logs in the fireplace.

11

Charity shrugged. "Well, you haven't eaten anything at all yet," she said.

Charity, a fragile doll, was wrapped in a large wine-coloured dressing gown, the sleeves folded back. Her hair was long, fat with curls, the colour of butter and honey. But her face was thin and pinched, her blue eyes looked too big.

"Something's happening," Charity said. She sat back in her chair.

"What's happening?"

"I don't know exactly. Something about you and the ghost of a girl in a pond. I heard Aurelia talking to Father and Galatea about it, just before breakfast. They said something was happening."

"What do you mean, Charity? Nothing happens. What could be happening?"

Galatea, the governess, was a formidable figure and Mercy feared her displeasure. And she wondered about her father. She hadn't seen him in a long time. She always knew he was nearby, probably working in his study, but he didn't feature in the regular pattern of the day. He was remote, and in the background.

"He sounded worried," Charity said. "What did you do? Aurelia was talking about you."

"I don't know," Mercy repeated. "What exactly did they say?"

What was the reason for the fuss? They were used to her seeing of ghosts. But not a new ghost, no. That was the reason

12

for worry. She felt it, in a shiver, from the top of her head to the soles of her feet.

Charity, an accomplished eavesdropper, raised her eyebrows, and smirked. She was infuriating. She opened her mouth to speak, but Aurelia marched in, with a tray and a tea service, also adorned with blue roses. Slices of toast were poised on a plate. She greeted Mercy and poured the girls each a cup of jasmine tea. She turned to poke at the fire and Charity stared at the wrinkle of steam rising from her cup.

"Just you wait and see," Charity whispered, lifting her eyes to Mercy. "It's all your fault." She picked up a spoon and tapped out a faint rhythm on the egg. She had her sly smile again. Mercy, pretending not to care, picked up a slice of warm toast and took a bite. Why did Charity have to pretend she knew everything?

Charity picked up the other slice, took one small bite, and put it back on the plate.

Later the girls waited in the library with their books for Galatea and their lesson. The room was very cold, without a fire. Mercy was anxious, expecting some kind of reprimand from the governess. The door opened.

"Father!" Mercy jumped to her feet. Trajan was standing in the doorway. She hadn't seen him for so long.

Charity looked up, and gave him a winning smile.

"Good morning, girls," he said, uncertainly. "I hope you are well."

He looked rather shabby and old. His white shirt and cravat were dingy and stained, and there were dark marks, like fingerprints, on his jacket. His hair hung in untidy black and iron-grey clumps. He sat down and stared at the girls, as though they were strangers, struggling to remember their names.

"Mercy. Charity," he said at last. Galatea stepped in beside him. She was an odd-looking woman. Ugly, maybe. And again, maybe not. Perhaps this was simply Mercy's view because the governess was so strict and unyielding. She had a beaky face. Her skin was dry and stretched, with a strong nose, a tall forehead and chestnut hair pulled back tightly.

Waiting for the scolding, Mercy stared at the sharp tips of Galatea's boots. Slowly she raised her eyes to the hem of the governess's plain black dress. Then the skirt, the tiny waist, her narrow, bony shoulders and, lastly – her face.

"Say good day to your governess, Mercy," Trajan said.

"Good day," Mercy squeaked.

"Good day, Galatea," Charity said sweetly. She tipped her head on one side, and smiled. Mercy twisted on her feet, bursting to speak to her father and not knowing what to say. She felt very shy, especially with Galatea standing over her. But she longed to talk, to find out where he had been and what he was doing. And why had he come to see them today? Galatea, too, stared at Trajan expectantly. He cleared his throat.

"Mercy, Charity," he said. "I have a concern. A worry. I'm

14

afraid the house faces some disruption, you see. It could be a problem for us." He spoke awkwardly.

"What do you mean, Father?" Charity said brightly.

"A disruption," he said again, struggling for the right word. "I want you to be careful. On your guard."

"On our guard for what?" Mercy said.

"For anything . . . strange. For the unexpected."

Mercy frowned. She remembered the snowdrop and the ghost. Presumably these were the unexpected things her father was talking about. How could they be dangerous?

The governess and the two girls waited for Trajan to speak again, but he coughed instead and thrust his hands into his pockets, already turning away.

"Remember what I told you," he said. "If anything concerns you, come and tell me." He was already reaching for the door.

"Where shall we find you?" Mercy called.

Trajan frowned. "Oh, here and there," he said, a vague gesture with his hand. "In the house." Then he was gone.

The girls and the governess stood for a moment in silence, Mercy puzzled by the warning.

"Well," Galatea said at last. "It's very cold in here today. Shall we find somewhere warmer to work?"

"The nursery parlour," Charity piped up. "Or the kitchen."

"The nursery parlour will be suitable," Galatea said. "We shall leave the kitchen to Aurelia, I think. Charity, will you lead the way?"

15

They studied Latin verbs and afterwards, Galatea taught them Italian, which Mercy could read well and speak poorly. Later they dined on venison pie with leeks and cabbage, and fresh bread still hot from the oven. Charity ate heartily, for once, but Mercy was haunted by strange thoughts, about her father and the snowdrop and the ghost in the pond. She wanted life to resume as it had been, before the intrusion.

As soon as the meal was over, Mercy went for her usual stroll in the gardens and then read with Charity by the fire. Then the girls ate supper with Galatea and Aurelia in the kitchen, and when the meal was finished Mercy went to her room, drew the curtains and shut the door. She curled up in bed with her favourite book, a fairy tale called *The Enchanter's Daughter*. On the title page her own name was inscribed beneath another name, her mother's. Thecla Arcadius Verga. Arcadius was her mother's maiden name. Her father said they had chosen English names for their daughters so they shouldn't feel out of place. This consideration seemed a little strange now.

The Enchanter's Daughter stood on a high balcony, above the snow, on a page edged with gold. Mercy mused, stroking the picture with her finger. The past was so far away. Today had been very strange. The winter had gone on and on. The weeks had flown by, one like another, but now everything was changing. A walk, a ghost, a father.

Just before dawn Aurelia helped her undress for bed and Mercy fell asleep, until Century's reverse morning, when Aurelia woke her up again.

16

"Mercy, dear, get up," Aurelia said. "Come on. Galatea wants to begin early today."

Mercy swung her legs out of bed and shook the hair from her eyes. Her head was heavy with dreams of brighter places. She dressed and ate her breakfast of boiled egg and toast with Charity. She took her cup to the kitchen, where Aurelia was baking bread. Mercy looked around, at the swags of dried herbs tied in bundles to the beams. Copper pans gleamed. The glass-fronted dresser was crammed with a huge dinner service, now never used. The familiar room seemed oddly new – if only because she was taking the time to look. When had she stopped noticing things?

Galatea collected them promptly. Charity was playing her usual role of diligent pupil. They studied Latin verbs, the governess picking up Mercy on every mistake, making her repeat her declensions time and again. Later, when Mercy was about to take her usual solitary stroll in the garden, Galatea decided they should all go together. Charity groaned, but Mercy was horrified.

"I want to go by myself – that's what I always do," Mercy said. "You can't come with me."

"You are not to be alone," Galatea said firmly. "I am following your father's orders. He said I should accompany you."

Mercy's heart was heavy. She had no pleasure so great as the walk on her own in the cold air and the moonlight. Galatea would crush her enjoyment. Mercy pursed her lips, choked with resentment.

Outside, the fields were sealed with frost, so they wrapped up in fur mittens, heavy coats and hats.

"Come along," Galatea said. They left through the kitchen, and headed out into the night. Moonlight glittered on the frozen grass. The glare burned in Mercy's face. So cold – even wrapped up. Charity grasped her sister's hand.

They walked through the rose garden and across the top of Distillery Meadow. Then Galatea led them through a gateway, and along a lane towards the tiny church at the top of the slope, just before the woods. Mercy had forgotten it was there. The family chapel. It was so quiet. Now and then a creature stirred in the icy undergrowth, disturbed by the tapping of three pairs of boots.

"Now, girls," Galatea said. "I think we should always walk out together after lessons. You both need some healthy exercise. It is too cold for sketching, but I wish you both to study the church, so we might recreate it in our drawings on our return to the house. You may choose any aspect you please."

She wore a pair of soft leather gloves, and a fox fur draped around her shoulders. The fox's mask was still intact, with sad amber eyes. Charity smiled at her, and skipped off at once, to the south side, studying the rounded yew trees, and the turrets. Mercy, who hated drawing, ambled reluctantly after her sister. Then – from a niche in the chapel wall – a barn owl floated, like a ghost. White and cream, soundless, the bird dropped from the night sky, and rose again, above the trees.

Mercy followed the bird, through the shadows under the yew trees, and past a solitary gravestone. Beyond the church, the trees rose up, thick and black. But a light caught her eye, a flicker of hot colour, in the east window. A flare beneath the stained glass made a glow behind the obscure pieces of blood red and royal blue glass. A candle. Someone was inside the church.

Mercy headed for the porch. She couldn't see Galatea and Charity, now obscured by the yew trees. She paused for a moment, in the shelter of the porch. She could smell the ancient stone. The flagstones were cold beneath her feet, even through her boots and stockings. She reached out her hand to the heavy door. Who could it be?

The door opened soundlessly, but the iron latch clacked when she let it go. Out of the moonlight it took a few moments for her eyes to adjust to the darkness. She walked into the main aisle, then she waited, one hand gripping the top of a pew. A single candle burned beneath a window on the east wall. A small circle of hot, yellow light flickered on the walls, and she saw the bent head of a man sitting at the end of a pew.

Mercy didn't know what to do. So she simply waited, and watched. The candle danced in the draught. She couldn't make out the picture in the window – the candlelight reflected only puzzle pieces of silver and grey. Then the man turned.

"Mercy," he said. The side of his face was shadowed, so she couldn't discern his features. He had a young man's voice. She shivered.

"Mercy," he said again. Slowly, she walked forward, moving her hand from pew to pew.

"I've been waiting for you," he said. A white face, with dark hair falling over his forehead. He was very strange, and handsome, like a prince in one of her antique volumes of fairy tales.

"Are you . . . ?" she said. "Are you—"

"A ghost? No."

"Then who are you?" Her voice trembled. She had forgotten how to speak to strangers. She straightened up, gathering her dignity.

"You saw the woman in the ice, didn't you?" he said.

"How do you know about her?"

They had both asked questions, and now both waited for an answer. The moment stretched.

"Who are you?" she repeated. The young man looked down and smiled. He swept the hair from his face.

"Claudius," he said.

"You are – family?" she said.

"I'm from the old country too," he said. "I am a Verga. Now, you answer my question. I think you saw the woman in the ice. A ghost."

"Yes," Mercy said. "Why don't you come to the house?"

"I sent you a message, Mercy. Did you find it, the snowdrop upon your pillow? I sent you to her. It's time, you see."

"It was you? You came into my room?" Mercy's heart beat

20

fast. "Time for what?" Now she was afraid, remembering her father's warning.

"Now I've come to see you," he said. "To help you."

"To help me? To help me do what? Where did you find the flower? They don't grow here." Mercy spoke loudly. It was too much to bear. Claudius put his finger to his lips.

"Galatea will hear," he said. "We don't have long."

"Do you know who she was, the ghost?"

Claudius responded with another question. "Do you know what happened to your mother, Mercy?"

"She died," Mercy said. "When I was younger." But as soon as the words left her mouth, she wondered. Her mother had died a long time ago. Though oddly, she could not remember a funeral, and now she thought about it, she didn't know where the grave was. Surely it would be here, at the family church? Should she look for it? Who had told her of Thecla's death? Had she made it up herself, a childish explanation for an absence? In her fairy tales, the mothers always died. She tried to remember – a pain she had long ignored now reawakened beneath her ribs.

"You can see her again, Mercy," Claudius said gently.

"How?" Mercy demanded. "Where is she?"

They were disturbed, then, by the sound of footsteps in the porch. The door began to open.

"Be careful, Mercy," Claudius whispered. "Do you understand? Do not trust what they tell you, your father and Galatea. Don't believe them." Then he slipped away, into the shadows at the back of the church. He vanished.

21

"Mercy?" Galatea stood in the doorway. "Who's there?"

"It's me," Mercy said. "The candle was burning. But no one's here."

Mercy was too far from the governess to make out her expression in the darkness, but Galatea's voice was sharp, maybe afraid.

"Come along, Mercy," she said. "We're returning to the house. I hope you have made some good observations for your sketch." She peered round the church, her face hawkish, before she closed the door behind them.

They marched home, the girls hurrying to keep up with the governess. Later, in the nursery parlour, Charity began to compose a sketch of the church and the yew trees. She was a talented artist – better than Mercy, even though she was younger. Mercy tried to draw the barn owl, but her thoughts were racing. Who was Claudius? Why was he trying to help her? Why should she not trust her own father? Claudius puzzled her, too. She didn't like to think of him stealing into her room as she slept. His appearance in the church had surprised her, but she couldn't help but feel there was something familiar about him. He had known who she was, and where to find her. Had they met before, a long time ago, when she was a little child? Perhaps he would find her again.

Galatea was not pleased with Mercy's half-hearted attempt at drawing the owl. She dismissed the girls, and retired to her own room. The sisters sat together, close to the fire, worn out by the lessons and the walk. Mercy was bursting with her news.

"Charity," she said. "I have something to tell you – a secret."

"A secret?" Her eyes lit up. "What is it?"

Mercy bit her lip. Perhaps it wouldn't be wise to tell Charity what had happened. Charity was Galatea's favourite and she was impulsive. She might tell the governess about Claudius. But the secret was too much for her to carry on her own.

"I saw someone – in the church. A man," Mercy said.

"Another ghost?"

"No, not a ghost. But Charity, he did look familiar, and the more I think about it, the more familiar he seems. He said his name was Claudius. And he said he was going to help us."

Charity frowned. "Help us do what? Where did he go? Galatea didn't say anything about anyone in the church, silly. We never see anyone."

"He disappeared, just as she came in."

Charity kicked her feet. "I think he sounds like one of your ghosts. If you were the only one who saw him. How do you know he wasn't?"

"He said he wasn't. Anyway – he didn't feel like a ghost. I can tell. And a candle was burning. Galatea saw it. Another strange thing – Claudius knew about the lady under the ice. He said he sent me to see her."

Charity didn't answer. She stuck out her stockinged toes and wiggled them in front of the fire.

"Mercy, life has become much more exciting, hasn't it?" she said. "Father talking to us and now your man. What's

23

happening to us? I feel like I've been asleep for ages. And now I'm really hungry!"

"I don't like it," Mercy said. "I don't like it at all. I want things to be the way they were."

Charity shrugged. She stood up and waltzed out of the room. But Mercy could not relax. Her thoughts were wound up tight, and she couldn't make any sense of what had happened. And why had she failed to mention to Charity Claudius's words about their mother?

II

Mercy was sleeping when she heard laughter in the corridor outside her bedroom. At first she couldn't distinguish whether the sound was part of a dream, or real. She woke, slowly, rising up and up through layers of dim, grey dreams. The laughter was like a slim golden banner, fluttering just ahead. She reached out her hand – but the banner was too far away. Up, up – she opened her eyes, and gasped. The room was dark, but the laughter was real. She heard it again. A child's laugh, full of life and delight.

Mercy had heard the sound often before. It was part of the morning, and so familiar she hardly noticed it any more, like the paintings she walked past, without seeing what was in the pictures. The laughter came from the ghost of a little girl, who ran up and down in the stretch of corridor outside her bedroom. She sounded happy and alive, and today her laughter had registered in Mercy's brain as she slept.

Properly awake now, Mercy sighed. So much of the detail

of life had faded from her awareness. Only now was she starting to notice things again. At her bedside the snowdrop was already wilting in a cup of water. Mercy climbed out of bed, carefully opened the door, and peeped out. There she was – the ghost. The girl looked about ten years old. She was dressed in a beautiful dress, decorated with pearls. Perhaps she was enjoying a wedding, or a special party, and that was why her moment of happiness had snagged in the corridor here, a time when she had been most herself.

Mercy smiled but she knew the ghost couldn't see her. The girl skipped. She appeared to be playing with someone Mercy couldn't see and she giggled. The ghost put her hands over her eyes and began to count. Hide-and-seek. But the ghost was peeking. She opened her fingers, spying through the chinks.

The ghost's invisible companion had obviously moved out of sight now, because the ghost lowered her hands. She twisted on her feet, looking one way and another, deciding where to go. Then she scampered away, into the darkness. Mercy had seen the girl so many times. The ghost ran through precisely the same motions, and made the same sounds. Only now it was Mercy who acted out of pattern. She followed the ghost along the corridor.

The ghost girl peered over her shoulder, looking for someone. She broke into a run, then walked again. She half skipped. She was enjoying herself, leading someone in a merry dance, playing a trick. Mercy hurried to keep up. The corridor was wide, leading along the main body of the house, at the front. Tall windows reared to her left, filled with stars. She didn't often come this way. Most of the house was closed up, inhabited by dust and spiders. The ghost disappeared momentarily, when a blaze of moonlight shone through her, putting her out. Then Mercy could see her again, further down, past the windows. She followed.

The little girl stopped by a wall hanging on the right wall. She looked through Mercy, who was now standing right beside her. How pretty she was, the ghost. Her skin was very pale, her eyelashes a light gold. The ghost seemed to hesitate by a wall hanging. She turned quickly, lifting a hand – then she was gone.

The house seemed to hold its breath for an instant. Mercy shivered, in a cold draught. Behind the wood panelling a mouse scratched. Mercy rubbed the top of her arms with her hands. Upon the tapestry a stag and a unicorn danced on their hind legs, either side of a blue and gold shield. The picture was covered in dust, tied to the wall with heavy cobwebs. Gingerly, Mercy stretched out her hand to brush off the dust.

"Mercy? Mercy!"

The sharp voice made her jump. Mercy snatched back her hand.

"You're late for breakfast, and Charity has already begun her lessons." It was Galatea, marching along the corridor. She stopped beside Mercy. "What are you doing here?" Galatea frowned, face heavy with suspicion.

Mercy swallowed nervously. Galatea was always scolding

27

her. Mercy knew she irritated the governess with her day-dreaming and carelessness. She didn't want to give Galatea more reason to grumble.

"Nothing," Mercy murmured. "Nothing. I was just – I was . . ." She didn't know what to say.

Galatea looked at the tapestry, then back at Mercy again.

"Are you looking for something?" she said.

Mercy shook her head. "I am sorry I'm late," she said. "I shall get dressed quickly." And without another word she went back to her room.

As she tugged on the dress, Mercy fretted over the events of the day before, and the suggestion by Claudius that she might see her mother again. How could that be, if her mother was dead? Buttoned up, Mercy stood straight. When had she stopped thinking about Thecla? When had she stopped missing her? Mercy tried to remember what had happened, but she couldn't even conjure up the memory of her mother's face. The knot of pain beneath her ribs squeezed tight. She closed her hands into fists, digging her nails into her palms. *The Enchanter's Daughter* lay on the floor by the bed, with the name inscribed in the front. Without the book, would she have forgotten her mother's name, too? She had to find out. On an impulse she tore out a piece of paper from her journal and scribbled a note to Claudius. Maybe she could leave it in the church.

Galatea called again and Mercy hurried to the parlour, to resume her Latin studies. Charity was smug, as she was already

28

hard at work when Mercy arrived, late and flustered. Mercy pulled her books open.

"Galatea said we should translate the poem on page one hundred and three," said Charity. "I've already completed the first verse. You will have to be quick to catch me up."

The governess called in briefly, to make sure they were working, but then disappeared again.

"She's talking to Father," Charity said.

"How do you know?"

"They are spending a lot of time together," Charity said. "Talking."

"How do you know?" Mercy repeated, more loudly. Her sister, in possession of a secret, was maddening.

"I've been following her," Charity said. "After our lessons, when you went to your room yesterday. I was hungry, so I went to the kitchen. And I saw her bustling along to Father's study."

"I expect she wanted to talk to him about our progress," Mercy said, trying not to sound curious.

"She spent two hours with him," Charity said. "It was almost bedtime when she left the room."

"You waited all that time?"

"No." Charity shook her head. "I left my bedroom door open, and listened for her return. I stepped out, made her jump. 'Galatea,' I said. 'I can't sleep. Will you read me a story?'"

Mercy's eyes widened. "What did she say?"

29

"Well, she looked quite excited. She smiled at me, but she said I was too old for bedtime stories. You don't suppose," Charity said archly, "that she's falling in love with Father?"

Mercy felt a curious constriction in her throat. The idea filled her with disgust. "A romance?" she whispered. "Father and Galatea?" Then louder: "No, of course not, you stupid girl! How could you suggest it! That is the most ridiculous thing I have ever heard. How could you imagine for a moment that Father could fall in love with that awful woman!"

She had to strangle the last word, because the woman herself stepped into the room. Mercy's face grew hot and red.

Galatea looked at them both.

"How is the translation coming along?" she asked. "Mercy? You haven't started. Come along! You are lazy today."

Mercy stared at the blank page in her exercise book.

"Yes, Galatea, I'm sorry," she mumbled. She focused on the poem. So many other thoughts kept bubbling up into her mind, making it hard to concentrate. But the poem was simple enough, and she finished it before Charity. The governess sat with them, supervising and making suggestions.

After lunch they walked together, right down to the lake. The water was very still and black. The margins were choked with brown bulrushes and a fringe of ice. Far away, ducks quacked.

The governess was quiet, but Charity chatted away to her merrily.

"Isn't it beautiful?" Charity said. "I'm sure there's an old temple somewhere on the other side, and a boathouse. It has been so long since we've walked here. In the summer, I think we used to take the boats out." Charity spun away, pirouetting on the frosty grass.

Mercy dragged ten paces behind, glowering at Galatea's upright back. It was strange to hear Charity talking about the past. Memories were stirring, for both of them. For too long their thoughts had followed a treadmill, thinking the same things over and over, their minds closing in and closing down. The arrival of Claudius had changed everything – thrown them all off kilter. Far away, on the moonlit water, a familiar ghost waved from a rowing boat. Waved and waved again.

Mercy wanted to get away on her own to the chapel, but Galatea seemed determined not to go near it again. Mercy hoped against hope that she might see Claudius, so she could ask him what he had meant. And if Galatea wouldn't take them to the chapel she would leave him the note somewhere else – somewhere private, away from Galatea's prying eyes. The boathouse, she remembered dimly, was just beyond a stand of horse chestnut trees, not far away.

As Charity chatted to Galatea, Mercy wandered off on her own. Of course it was stupid to think Claudius, magically, would be waiting for her, but she still hurried. The horse chestnuts stood on a landscaped hump. The trees were much taller and grander than she remembered. On the other side, the boathouse perched over the water on stilts. She walked up the ramp on the landward side, and tried the arched door. It was locked. Mercy sighed, and stepped back. The boathouse needed a coat of paint. The stilts were dark and corroded. Here and there planks were warped or eaten away.

Mercy took the note from her pocket. She had folded the paper, and written a name on it. It was foolish to leave it here. But Galatea was already suspicious about the church. And if Claudius was spying on them, he would find the letter.

"Mercy! Where are you?" Charity was shouting. Quickly Mercy slipped the letter underneath the boathouse door, so it was half sticking out. Then she ran back through the horse chestnuts to find Charity waiting for her.

"Where's Galatea?" Mercy asked.

"She's gone ahead, back to the house. She's looking for you! Where did you disappear to?"

"Nowhere," Mercy shrugged. "I was just looking at the lake."

"Come on," Charity urged. "We'll catch her up. Before she gets cross."

They began to run towards the house, but Charity tired quickly and they soon slowed to a walk.

"Galatea said we were all to dine together tonight – with Father too," said Charity.

"In the kitchen?"

"No silly, in the dining room."

"The dining room," Mercy whispered, remembering crowds of candles, the dinner service. "Why?" she said.

"Maybe Father wants to dine with her," Charity said.

"I don't believe it. Why is he changing things? I thought he didn't want any disruption."

"Galatea said he wants to keep an eye on us too – to find out what's going on. Maybe he just wants to talk with us. And Galatea. Like a family."

Mercy chewed the inside of her cheek. Why couldn't Charity be serious, instead of teasing her about Trajan and Galatea? Wasn't she worried about the changes taking place, about their father's warnings?

Of course Galatea and Aurelia were part of the family. They both came from Italy and carried the Verga name, but they were poorer relatives, obliged to be servants. While Aurelia might love the two young daughters of the house, she was bound to obey the orders of the master, and so was Galatea. Perhaps it was time for Mercy to rid her sister of the irritating distraction of a romance between Trajan and the governess and enrol her help in finding out more about their mother. It was a risk, because Charity was impetuous, but Mercy longed for someone to share her thoughts. She took a deep breath.

"What about Mother?" she said. The word seemed to hang on the air.

"Mother?" Charity repeated. "What about her?"

"Do you know where she is?"

"She died. When we were young. What do you mean?"

"Then where is she buried? At the chapel? Do you remember the funeral? Surely they would have taken us to our mother's funeral, even if we were young. And how did she die? She wasn't old."

Charity frowned. "I don't remember," she said.

Bravely, Mercy ploughed on. She took the bit between her teeth. "Claudius told me I could see her again."

"Claudius? Your church ghost?"

"He wasn't a ghost! I told you."

They walked side by side, closer together.

"Do you remember her face?" Mercy asked, eager now. "Can you conjure it up, in your mind?"

Charity shook her head. "No," she said. "I remember a feeling. That's all."

"Nor can I. Don't you think that's strange?"

Charity looked stunned. They walked on together in silence and Charity turned her face away from her sister, closing herself off. When Charity spoke again, minutes later, her voice was choked.

"Why did you make me think of Mother?" she said. "I haven't thought about her for such a long time. I didn't even remember that I missed her."

Mercy pressed on. "Do you remember a funeral?" she repeated.

Face down, Charity shook her head. "I don't remember anything about her," she said. "That isn't right, is it? She's our mother. Why don't we think about her or talk about her?"

"What if she isn't dead?" Mercy persisted.

"We've got to find out," Charity said. "We need to know.

34

At dinner tonight – with Father. He won't be able to get away. I shall ask him. I want to know."

Before Mercy could reply, Charity began to run again. Mercy shouted out, but Charity ignored her.

Back at the house, Charity locked herself in her room, and she wouldn't answer when Mercy knocked and cajoled.

Mercy sat upon her own bed and worried. What was Charity going to say? How stupid she'd been, to tell her, to stir it up. In a state of agitation Mercy pulled at her hair. She was afraid of Trajan's response.

They did not dine till late. Galatea collected Mercy. Aurelia had been summoned to fasten her into a formal dress and pin up her hair. Charity waited in Galatea's wing, studiously avoiding Mercy's silent entreaties, keeping close beside the governess.

How pale Charity looked, and her eyes were red, as though she had been crying. Mercy felt an uneasy twinge of guilt, for upsetting her sister with questions about their mother.

Aurelia had set four places at one end of the long table in the dining room. Trajan was waiting, dressed in a long jacket, less worn but rather more dusty than usual. He had brushed his hair from his face. His hands, protruding from frayed silk cuffs, were very thin and clean. Red cufflinks, rubies perhaps, blinked in the candlelight.

"Sit down, sit down," he said. Mercy thought he looked nervous and uncomfortable.

They dined on tender roast beef, and roast potatoes. The girls were allowed a sip of red wine, to taste. The atmosphere was subdued. Galatea talked with Trajan about life in the old country. Mercy understood none of it. They may as well have been talking about another world. Then Charity chattered about their lessons. Mercy brooded silently, picking at her food, studying Galatea. The situation felt entirely wrong. It had been easy to half sleep through the days, without all these odd thoughts firing up in her mind. Now she had so many questions. Her body ached, as though old forgotten bruises were rising in her bones. She had an urge to jump up and shout out. Instead, she took a breath and swallowed everything down. She placed her cutlery upon the plate.

Aurelia served a treacle pudding for dessert, with a fragrant almond custard, but Mercy couldn't eat it.

"Father," Charity said, finally placing her fork upon her dish. "I've been meaning to ask you something."

She had been charming him in readiness for this moment. Mercy stiffened, anticipating trouble, but Trajan was quite unprepared for the question to follow.

"What happened to our mother?"

Galatea coughed abruptly.

"I can hardly remember her," Charity continued. "I had always imagined she had died, but Mercy said she didn't go to the funeral. She *did* die, didn't she?"

Mercy stared at her father. His face had altered subtly, a

curious yellow tinge rising in his cheeks. She saw his fingers whiten as he gripped his glass.

The governess coughed again.

Mercy stared at Trajan's hand. He was pressing so hard. The glass collapsed. He opened his fingers to reveal blood and wine and sharp fragments in the skin of his palm.

"Charity," Galatea said. "Don't ask your father about these things. Can't you see it upsets him? I will speak with you later."

Trajan stood up abruptly. "Thank you for joining me," he said to his daughters. "It has been too long. We shall eat together again soon. I must – I must clean my hand."

He walked stiffly from the room, knocking a side table as though he couldn't see. When the door had closed behind him, Charity picked up her fork again, and started to hum.

"Charity!" Galatea snapped. "Be quiet. Keep still. Can't you see how you have saddened your father?"

"I only asked," Charity said, peering up through long eyelashes. "She was my *mother*. Surely I'm allowed to know what happened to her? Will you tell me?"

The governess pursed her lips. She paused for a moment, thinking. "Your mother died," she said. "Some years ago."

"*How* did she die? Why didn't we go to a funeral?"

"She died while travelling abroad, in the old country. She became ill, and she was buried there. That is why you didn't go to a funeral, because you were here at Century. I understand your lives have not been . . . ideal."

Mercy lifted her head. She knew Galatea was lying from the tone of her voice. She remembered the warning from Claudius not to believe her. Now she felt his words had been confirmed. Her mother hadn't died in the old country, she was sure of it.

"Do you know if there is a portrait of my mother?" she asked quietly.

"I think there was," Galatea said. "Your father was so heartbroken when she died, he had all the pictures put away, and he closed up most of Century. This was so much her house, you see."

"How long ago did Mother die? How old was I?" Mercy spoke slowly. She thought she was twelve now but she could no more remember a last birthday than she could recall the funeral.

"A long time ago," Galatea said. "I don't know exactly how long. Now – that is enough. No more questions tonight. We shall retire to the nursery parlour and you can continue with your embroidery until bedtime."

Sitting beside the friendly fire, Mercy stitched the petals of a white flower by candlelight. The painstaking work soothed her mind. Charity, on the other side of the fire, had her feet up on a stool, and she stared at the flames, sighing from time to time. Galatea, between them, succumbed to Charity's demands for a story and read a folk tale about a goose girl who didn't cast a shadow.

When the story was over, Mercy said good night, and returned to her bedroom. Before she undressed she retraced her steps past the tall windows to the stag-and-unicorn tapestry. There was something strange about it, but she couldn't work out what. She fumbled behind the hanging, but she found only cobwebs. Then she returned to her room, confused and dispirited. She sat at her desk and wrote in her journal, long pages about her resentment of Galatea, the questions about her mother, and her uncertainty about her own age. Then she hid the book beneath a floorboard, under her bed. When she undressed the sky was pale in the east. Night's retreating petticoats, she thought. She drew the curtains, and lay down in bed.

Someone shouted out. A scream—

Mercy woke with a start. Night had fallen.

She jumped out of bed and ran to the door. Who was it? The voice was so familiar. Not Charity, no. Someone else . . .

She opened the door. The ghost. The girl in the corridor – she had broken the endless game of hide-and-seek. She was frightened now, standing still, staring at something. Mercy hurried towards her.

"What is it?" she said. The ghost couldn't see her but it seemed to look right into her eyes. The girl screamed again. Then she turned on her heels and ran away, little feet flying, hair in a stream. Mercy hurried after. The ghost took the familiar path, to the tapestry – then she seemed to disappear right through the wall. Mercy was close behind. She wanted to follow – so much she wanted to follow. She thrust her hand past the unicorn, into empty space. A doorway, now without a door. Seizing the moment, Mercy pushed through.

For a few long moments, she couldn't see anything. She was swallowed up. An intense cold, the ground falling away. How long was the space between one heartbeat and the next? How far does the blood flow in the space between the heart's hammer blows? The stars drummed. The night uncoiled . . .

The light!

A blast of sunlight. The unrelenting force of it crashed over her, sent her reeling.

She stumbled back against shelves, leaning upon them, covering her face with her hands. She wasn't used to it, the blaze of daylight, the heat.

Slowly Mercy adjusted. She peeked through the chinks in her fingers, as the ghost had done, cheating at hide-and-seek. Such lurid, painful colours. She was standing in the library, near the geographical treatises and maps. The room was familiar. Mercy lowered her hands. She stared at her fingers. The cruel light picked out every tiny hair, the tracery of tender veins. The sun was hard like a hammer. She could not look directly at the window, so she edged around the room to the door.

The library did look different. The books were bright and new, the floorboards polished. Books lay open on a table, with letters and papers. The place looked used – it looked alive.

This wasn't what she had expected. A secret passageway perhaps – leading to a hideaway where the ghost girl had waited for her friend. Or hidden from her pursuer, the last time, when she had screamed and run away.

Mercy opened the library door and crept out. She walked along the corridor, noting the faces of her ancestors on the walls, the paintings altered by the light. A mirror loomed unexpectedly, granting her a quick glimpse of a strange white face in a flood of untidy black hair.

Mercy reached the nursery parlour in the sunlit Century. Someone was coming out of the door and she stepped back, out of the way.

A tall, curvaceous woman in a red silk dress walked straight past her. The woman had long golden hair. Mercy shrank back, but the woman didn't seem to see her. Mercy caught the scent of her perfume, which trailed behind the woman like a ribbon. The scent, like spice and flowers, touched on memories in forgotten places. Mercy stood against the wall in the corridor, her heart thumping. She drew another breath, trying to capture the last fading threads of the perfume. Was it her? Was that her mother, Thecla, the woman Galatea had told her was dead? And if it was her mother, why couldn't she remember her? Why wasn't she sure?

The woman was soon out of sight. Mercy gathered her thoughts and followed her, up a stairway to the next floor, and into a bedroom.

Perhaps, in this altered version of Century, in the strange light, Mercy was a ghost. The woman looked right through her, and acted with the ease of someone who believes they are entirely alone. The light was not too bright here, with muslin curtains partially drawn across the window. The bed was large, carved from dark, heavy wood, with wreaths of oak leaves and acorns crowning the headboard. The woman sat at a dressing table, crowded with glass pots, brushes and pretty card boxes. She was searching through the drawers, where dozens of letters were piled. Bolder now, Mercy stepped closer, until she was just behind her.

The woman rifled through the letters, but she couldn't find what she was looking for. Mercy hovered over her, taking in the details of her dress, the silver chain fastened around her neck. She had to be Thecla, surely. Mercy ached to speak with her, to hear her voice, but the woman stood up, with a sigh, and marched back out of the room and down the stairs. Mercy tried to follow but the house was playing tricks and the corridors seemed to run away and recede. She couldn't keep up.

Mercy returned to the nursery parlour, where two girls were sitting at the table. She sidled into the room. The sound of the door opening caused the dark-haired girl to look up. The girls were drinking tea, reading, and talking. Books lay open upon the table. The teacups were painted with blue roses. The fireplace was filled with an arrangement of dried flowers and pinecones, but the air was still warm – and fragrant. The parlour window was wide open, and the air carried the scent of grass and fresh leaves, the perfume of flowers from the garden, the scent of the roses. Summer. Long ago, far away summer.

But the sun still hurt. So she moved away from the window,

and perched on the little chair in the corner of the room. It was a child's chair, too small for her. Her own nursery parlour had one just the same, though a little more threadbare. When she moved, the dark-haired girl looked up again, as though she had noticed a change in the light. She wrinkled her brow. "Are you cold?" she said.

"No, not at all. In fact I am rather hot," the fair girl said, tugging at her collar.

"I felt a chill," the dark girl said. She gave a convincing little shiver, as though to demonstrate.

Mercy studied them, fascinated. The girls were Charity and herself, aged about eight and ten. Only these little girls were rosy with health, and she saw little Charity's arms were round and plump. They chattered and laughed. With a curious pang, Mercy realised she couldn't remember the last time she had laughed. And the girls were so heedless of the warm, delicious touch of the sun, which brought out the gold in little Charity's hair. How she envied them. Why had this been taken away from her? Once, once Mercy had lived so, in the golden light and the heat.

The girls resumed their studies, little Charity kicking her feet in the air carelessly. Little Mercy read aloud a poem she had written, about a water nymph in a river who fell in love with a demon in a black rock. Little Charity laughed, then read aloud her own piece, about an enchanted dress that carried its wearer to a fairyland ball, where the wearer was obliged to dance for a hundred years, since one night in the other world was the equivalent of a century in her own. Mercy could see her younger self was moved by her sister's poem – and jealous too.

"It's beautiful," little Mercy said, glowering. "Beautiful and sad. I can imagine her coming home, her feet in ribbons, her dress in rags, to find everyone she knew had died long before."

"Paint a picture," little Charity said, lowering her eyes, acknowledging the praise. "Paint it for me."

Then they were tidying up. Mercy felt a little dazed. The shadows were shifting on the wall, stretching out. Finally they were gone, the two girls. The teacups had gone too, though Mercy had not noticed anyone coming in to collect them.

Mercy left the parlour to find the summer version of her own room. No one was there. Mercy briefly perused the items on the dressing table – hairbrush, perfume bottle, the dish of soap and towel. The jug and bowl on the floor were the same.

"Mercy," a faraway voice called. "Where are you?"

It was Galatea, doubtless calling little Mercy for some telling off. The irritant tone of her voice hadn't changed. But Mercy began to worry. Perhaps in her own dark Century Galatea was also looking for her. How would she get back?

Mercy hurried to the library. Now Trajan was sitting at a desk, with a book. He looked so much younger; smooth-skinned, his hair entirely black. She walked towards him, hesitating, hardly believing he wouldn't see her. But Trajan was engrossed in his book and turned a page without registering her presence at all. Mercy stared. He looked like

44

another man, with his clean, strong hands; decision and vitality written in the lines of his body.

Beside the book Trajan was reading, he had another volume – a romance of some kind. A novel bound in fine red leather, embossed with gold leaf. Mercy saw the book was called *Century*. She picked it up, her hands shaking, but Trajan didn't seem to notice. She turned to the first page, a picture, a black-and-white sketch of a house standing in the snow, the light reflecting off the windows, while a man on a horse galloped away.

The author's name, written on the front page, was Trajan Quintus Verga, with the date: 1790.

Her father had written a book about the house.

She sensed something curious about this book. Like herself, it didn't quite belong in this summer place, in the past. It vibrated slightly in her hands, charged with energy. The words seemed to swarm over the paper.

She flicked through the pages of the book with a sense of urgency. The words passed in a blur. She recognised her father's handwriting but she couldn't get a sense of the story. One page drew her up short. She stared. Another picture. A fine sketch of a young man, the style elongating and narrowing his features, but undoubtedly it was him: Claudius. So that much was true. He was a part of the family, and maybe she had known him, once.

She glanced at the picture again. Could she take the book? She carried the red book to the shelves where the maps were piled. Yes, this was the place she had arrived. But how to get back?

She cleared her mind, and willed a return. Then something pulled her, from behind. She was tugged back and upwards, into a long, dark space. A mineshaft, a magic well. Up and up, her hair flying.

She landed with a soft thump.

Mercy opened her eyes cautiously. It was still dark. She was sitting on the floor in the corridor by the tapestry.

Galatea was standing further down, outside her bedroom.

"Just a moment," Mercy called out. "You woke me up, just a moment."

Her arms were still crossed tightly against her chest, but the book was gone.

Galatea marched down. "Woke you up?" she said. "What were you doing, sleeping on the floor?"

"I don't know," Mercy said, struggling to her feet. Her mind was dazed, reeling from the journey and the unexpected images of the past.

The governess put one cold, hard hand on Mercy's forehead, and pursed her pale lips. The skin puckered about her mouth, tiny seams in the skin. For a moment Galatea looked very old.

"You seem to have a slight fever," she said at last. "You will be excused lessons this morning. Stay in your room. I will ask Aurelia to bring up some breakfast for you here."

"I'm fine," Mercy protested. "I don't feel in the slightest bit

46

ill." She didn't want to be shut away on her own this morning – she had to talk to Charity.

But Galatea marched Mercy to her bedroom and forbade her to get out of bed. Then she hurried away down the corridor. Mercy struggled to gather her thoughts. More questions, and more. She felt she was falling to pieces. The discovery of the little family was a shaft of sunlight in the prison of the winter day. How long ago had that been? What year was it now? And she had seen Thecla, she was sure of it. Mercy felt so far away from her mother, in this winter place, and she longed to see her again.

And the book called *Century*. She sensed its importance, its power. What was it? And why did it contain a picture of Claudius? When would she see him again?

III

Mercy crept along the corridor, past the door. Inside she could hear Charity's neat, clear voice reading a poem in Latin. Every now and then Galatea's deeper voice would interrupt. Mercy was nervous. Of course she wasn't ill. Galatea just wanted to stop her talking to Charity. Mercy had screwed up her courage to disobey. She would have to find Claudius again. She hurried along the corridor, tiptoed down the stairs, and carefully lifted the latch on the kitchen door. She did not want Aurelia to see her either.

The kitchen was warm from the fire. The housekeeper wasn't in sight – perhaps she was fetching coal. The insubstantial cat drowsed on top of the dresser. A mound of dough waited on the table, coated in flour. Mercy scanned the room again – then ran across the flagstones to the back door, and out, into the night garden.

The cold air swallowed her – took her breath away. The grass was coated with frost, the trees were bare, cased in ice.

Dead leaves glittered. Mercy picked up her skirts. She took one last look at the house, where the candlelight burned so warmly in the kitchen window, then she ran again, out of the garden and down the long slope to the lake. She was out of breath when she stopped, at the water's margin. The ice had spread, a white and silver lid upon the lake. Far out, the black shapes of ducks perched unhappily. The moon rose above the trees, beyond the lake.

Mercy shaded her eyes from the moon's glare to scan the lakeside for movement. The ghost in the rowing boat waved, and waved again. She headed for the boathouse. Her letter had disappeared.

Mercy pushed the door. This time it swung open, with a sound like a sigh. "Hello?" she called quietly. "Claudius, are you there?"

No one answered, so she pushed the door further. It was very dark inside. A little moonlight reflected on the ice below, where a boat was moored.

"Claudius?" she called again. The boathouse was empty. Someone had been here surely – taken the letter and left the door unlocked. But who? And didn't the air retain some faint residual warmth, as though they had been here only a short time ago? Mercy clutched the rail overlooking the ice-floor and the rowing boat. A bird had left an old, untidy nest in it.

The door slammed shut. Mercy nearly tumbled over the rail.

"Shhh," Claudius said. He stood by the closed door, his finger raised to his lips. "I wanted to talk to you. I followed you down from the house," he said.

"Did you find my letter?" Mercy demanded.

"What letter?"

"I left you a letter here – under the door."

"No," he said. "If it's gone, someone else has taken it."

"Then how did you know to find me here?"

"As I said – I followed you down from the house. I've been waiting for a chance to speak with you."

He sat upon the bench by the wall.

"Here," he said, patting the space beside him. "They'll be looking for you soon. We don't have much time."

Mercy sat down, cautiously.

"Who are you?" she said. "I saw a picture of you – in a book. And the book was called Century, like the house."

Claudius brushed the hair back from his face. "I'm part of the history of the house," he said.

"So you're a ghost?"

"No, not a ghost. I'm as much alive as you," he said. He grasped her hand. His hand was much warmer than her own. His fingers burned.

"See," he said. "Not a ghost."

Mercy pulled her hand away. "So how do you know about me? How do you know about the ghosts?"

"Because you're part of the history of the house too," he said. "Once we were friends."

51

Mercy shook her head. "It might be true," she said. "But I don't remember it."

"I want to set you free, Mercy," he said. "Your father and his servants want to keep you in the dark." His eyes shone, in the darkness of the boathouse. Again one half of his face was shadowed, the other half illuminated by the pale light.

"Keep me in the dark?"

"I came here to find you. I took you a snowdrop, as a message – a signpost to the pond in Distillery Meadow," Claudius said. "Now you must see the ghost again. It's time for you to wake up. Pick up all the pieces, Mercy. Put them all together again and find out the truth about your mother."

"I don't understand," Mercy said.

"I will see you again soon," he said, looking around anxiously, peering out of the door. "I can't stay long. Speak to the ghost. I sent you to her. She will help you."

He stepped out of the boathouse. Mercy stood up. By the time she reached the doorway Claudius had disappeared.

Mercy didn't know how much time she had left. When Charity stopped her lessons for a break, Galatea would check her room. Perhaps they already knew she had gone out. But she had to see the ghost in the pond. Distillery Meadow was some twenty minutes' walk from the lake, if she hurried. Her head rattled with thoughts as she took long, tiring strides. She wasn't quite sure that she trusted Claudius. Did he come from the other, brighter place? The Century she had visited? The Century, perhaps, where the ghosts came from?

At the top of the hill, Mercy hurried through the gardens, and out again, on the other side, where the meadow fell away. Her face was damp and hot. She took off her hat, baring her head to the cold air.

The pond – the meadow's black pocket. It was a small, deep hole where the water drained from the fields. In the spring, she remembered distantly, there were flowers and coal-black moorhen chicks. How long ago was spring?

Mercy loosened her scarf, and sat down on the cold roots of a hawthorn tree, by the pond. She wondered if the ghost would reappear. That first time, the woman had glided under the ice in the light just before sunrise. But dawn was many hours away. Mercy waited. She pulled her hat on again over her ears, and stamped around the pond impatiently. She imagined the fuss in the house, Aurelia and Galatea looking for her.

"Come on," she muttered under her breath. "Come and see me."

The moon was higher now. Far off, a fox barked in an overgrown hedgerow. Mercy stepped down, closer to the pond. She prodded the ice with her toe. The surface was pitted and bubbled, with veins of frozen weed. It would be hard to see through. Mercy leaned over, and rubbed off the frost with her gloved hand.

The face stared up.

The sight was so sudden and close that Mercy jumped back. The white face was only inches from her own, its empty eyes vacant. Mercy took a deep breath, and another, steeling herself to look again into the empty eyes. Then she crept forward again and lay on the hard ground on her stomach, and leaned over the pond. The ghost was still there – a beautiful young woman, her hair a dark, drowned green in the water. Her lips were white. Her mouth opened and closed, as though she were speaking, but Mercy couldn't hear what she said.

"Claudius sent me," Mercy said. "You have to tell me something. You have to explain."

The ghost's mouth moved again, but the words were stuck under the ice.

"I can't hear you," Mercy said, banging the ice with her fist. "I might not get another chance."

The ghost looked sad now. The blank eyes reflected something – a flash of sea-blue, a glimmer of life rising up. Then the ghost streamed away, her face disappearing, the white dress swirling in the underwater current. She drifted across the pond.

"Don't go!" Mercy shouted. "Don't go yet. You have to help me."

The ghost didn't listen. The billow of the dress faded too, and the pond was still. The disappointment was crushing, after nerving herself to speak to the ghost. She had no idea who the young woman was. Why did she haunt the pond? Had she drowned? Mercy shuddered, imagining the cold of the water, the lid of ice sealed across. Maybe Claudius would tell her the name of the girl in the pond.

Mercy stood up, the charge of emotion falling flat. Her energy seemed to drop away all at once. Cold crept into her fingers. She thought about the long walk home. Maybe they haven't even noticed I've gone, she thought. It was a vain hope.

Then she noticed something glitter, at the frozen fringes of the pond. Curious, she walked around the bank and peered through the cloudy ice. She took off her gloves and rubbed at the surface with her fingers, trying to see what it was. There – beneath the ice – a silvery shining. Mercy tried punching the surface of the pond but the ice was thick and stubborn. So she stamped on it, hard, with the heel of her boot. The ice cracked, with a sound like a gun shot. She stamped again, breaking through to the shallow water near the bank. Water soaked through her leather boot, shockingly cold. Mercy dug her hand into the water, grazing her fingers on the broken shards of ice. Mud swirled, obscuring the water.

Three rusty keys on a ring. She drew them out of the water, triumphant. One was larger than the others – a door key, perhaps. Mercy smiled.

"Thank you," she said aloud, to the ghost. "Thank you very much."

Mercy stowed the keys in a pocket underneath her coat. She would be in trouble – but now she had something to show for it.

Galatea awaited Mercy, her face like thunder. The governess could hardly bring herself to speak to her charge. Carrying a single candle, she led Mercy through the house, away from the kitchen and the familiar rooms where Mercy and Charity spent their countless days. They walked down musty corridors Mercy had forgotten existed, passed doorways into rooms she might once have visited, a long time ago. Paintings loomed, with landscapes and faces she dimly remembered. Mercy was anxious, but her momentary despair at the side of the pond had dispelled. The keys were a hope to clutch on to.

Galatea opened a door in a panelled wall and they entered a drawing room, with a chandelier looped in cobwebs.

Mercy hung back, staring at the grey rags of the webs, the dim glint of the glass drops in the candlelight.

"Come along," Galatea chided. She pulled back a curtain and opened another door.

Mercy looked up, a memory stirring. She had a vague recollection of this place. What did it lead into? An image flashed in her mind; a roof of glass, a jungle of emerald leaves. Yes – the great conservatory – once Trajan's pride and joy.

"Mercy!" Galatea called sharply.

Mercy trotted after the trim, severe figure of the governess, who held the curtain from the door so Mercy might pass through. Then Galatea left her.

The conservatory lay before her. The light was very bright, the moon burning overhead like a torch. The glasshouse ran along Century's south side, the floor tiled with chequers of black and white. Fans of glass were held in ribs of white wood, but the glass was grimed with lichen, spots of green mould and bird droppings.

Once, huge tropical ferns had pressed against these glass walls. Vines and shrubs from rainforests had run rampant, blossoming with flowers like paper, like silk, warmed by the hothouse stoves. Now, everything was dead.

Slowly Mercy descended the three steps, pushing her way through dry, black branches overhanging the path. The conservatory looked so much bigger, because the plants had shrivelled and fallen away. Here and there, a handful of mummified leaves still littered the floor. Giant pots held quantities of lifeless, powdery soil.

She remembered . . . once upon a time, weren't there butterflies in the hothouse? Butterflies as big as crows, and hummingbirds, tiny as her little finger.

Trajan was sitting at an ornate iron table, absurdly civilised amongst the wreckage of his plants. He looked frail, like an old man. He lifted his face as Mercy drew near.

"Mercy," he said gently. "Sit down."

She perched on the chair next to his. He nodded.

"I walked here, last night," he said. "I spent so many years tending the plants, and now they are all dead. We used to grow peaches and apricots at Century. They were remarkable. Delicious." He fell silent for a moment, looking into a distance Mercy couldn't see. Then he sighed.

"I don't have an appetite these days," he said. "And you look very thin."

Mercy didn't know what to say. Trajan had kept himself at such a distance for so long. He wasn't a part of the sisters' repeating winter lives, except as a shadow moving dimly in the background.

Trajan was quiet again. He had lost the habit of speaking. Mercy waited. So many questions jostled in her mind, but she couldn't bring herself to ask them, afraid he might stop talking altogether. She understood her adventures were an irritation to him. An annoyance. Angrily, and abruptly, she turned away from Trajan and stared into the ruins of the ornamental pond. Once, under leaves like flags, giant fish had swum in slow circles, like jewels, ruby, amber and silver. Now the pond was a cracked and empty bowl, muddy and green-stained.

"Mercy," he said reluctantly. "Galatea is very angry with you."

No, not Galatea, Mercy thought. *You* are angry with me. Galatea does as you tell her.

Mercy resented him shifting the anger to Galatea, as though it were nothing to do with him. But she didn't want him to be cross either. He looked as though any seizure of emotion would snap him in two.

"I know," Mercy said. "I went out when she told me to stay in bed. But I wasn't ill. I wasn't! I just wanted some fresh air – to clear my head."

Trajan looked directly into her face. His eyes were so blue.

"I don't wish to hear your excuses, Mercy," he said gravely. "I committed you to Galatea's care, and you must obey her. This is not the kind of behaviour I expect of you."

"But Father – I have so many questions," she plunged on.

"Mercy!" he interrupted. "I won't hear any more. Change has come upon us but we must fight it – for our own protection. I understand a malign influence is at work in the house, causing disruption; and I will resist it. Galatea has my absolute confidence, and I expect you to treat her with the respect she deserves."

"Why do we need protecting?" she tried again. "I don't wish to upset you, but – can't you tell me anything about my mother? I remember her so little. I can't even imagine her face. Is there a picture of her?"

Trajan looked at the backs of his hands. The colour in his eyes seemed to cloud. She sensed the ending of their moment of intimacy. He drew back.

"The pictures are locked away," he said. "I can't bear to see them, Mercy. Go away now. Join your sister in the parlour for lunch."

Mercy stood up slowly.

"Mercy?" he called out, as she walked away. "I am glad to hear you are not ill, after all," he said.

She went back to the drawing room where Galatea was sitting at the table with her candle.

"I am sorry," Mercy said. Galatea stood up, and sniffed.

They dined together, and afterwards, alone in the nursery parlour Mercy repeated to Charity what Trajan had told her.

"How old are you, Charity?"

Charity's eyes narrowed. She hesitated. "Ten, I think," she said.

"But you're not certain. Don't you think that's strange?"

"I don't know," Charity said. "I hadn't really thought about it before."

"Don't you wonder why we never see the day?"

"No," Charity said.

"But we used to, I'm sure," Mercy ploughed on. "I can remember. I think I remember."

The past stirred, unfolding forgotten places in her mind. Like a book she had abandoned on the shelf, the pages of her memory now fluttered at random, casting snatches of a forgotten story into light.

When the dishes were cleared and Aurelia had bustled away, Charity took out some books.

"We're to write an account of the Danes' invasion of Wessex in the ninth century," she announced. "Galatea has left us books to read."

"How dull," Mercy yawned. She felt very tired now, the earlier exertion catching up. How could she think about the Danes now?

"It's not so dull," Charity said. "I've started, you see, while you were being scolded by Father. It's King Alfred, living in the marshes on the Somerset levels."

She lifted up her note-book, to show how much she had already written. Then she looked very serious. "Where did you go this morning?"

"I went to the lake," Mercy said.

"Why did you run away?"

"I didn't run away. I just wanted some fresh air, to clear my head."

"Galatea thinks you're up to something. She and Aurelia went to see Father, while I was supposed to be studying, but I sneaked out and listened to them talking. You're not the only one interested in unravelling mysteries."

"What did they say?"

"You tell me – and I'll tell you."

It was quite possible for Charity to be sweet as pie for the governess one minute – while spying on her the next.

"I saw Claudius again," Mercy said. "At the boathouse. But you mustn't tell anyone! He said he wants to help us – and they'll try and stop him. Now, what did Galatea say?"

"Galatea thinks you have fallen under a malevolent influence," Charity said. "That's what she said. Malevolent – something bad. And I think that must be Claudius, don't you?"

"I know what malevolent means," Mercy said, irritated. "What else did she say? What did Father say?"

"Well, they think Claudius is making the changes happen in the house. I don't know how. We are waking up, that is what Father said. He referred to our questions about Mother, remembering the past. He's worried that with your special talents you've been exploited by Claudius and that he is trying to hurt us."

"Now you tell me the rest," Charity said. She stared at Mercy. "Why did Galatea tell you to stay in your room?"

But Mercy could hear steps in the corridor. "After bedtime," she whispered. "Come to my room."

When they were supposed to be reading and settling down to sleep, Mercy went to Charity's room instead. She drew out the keys from her pocket.

"Keys," Charity said. "What are they for?"

"I think they open our mother's room."

Charity's face became very still. She looked away from Mercy for a moment, and fixed her eyes on the wall. Then she said: "Where did you get them?"

Mercy sat on the edge of her sister's bed and quickly described the doorway into the past, the sunshine, the woman dressed in red.

Charity was very pale now. "Can I go too?" she said. "I want to see her."

"I don't know," Mercy said. "I haven't worked out how the doorway works."

"I want to try. Take me now," Charity said.

They hurried along the corridor to the tapestry and Charity pressed and banged against the wooden panelling. But the way remained closed. Charity's eyes filled with tears but she bit them back. She shook her head and pressed her hands together.

"Can we find Mother's room?" she said quickly.

Mercy had rubbed the keys with a piece of rag, and scratched at them with her fingernails. Still they were pocked with rust. She wondered how long they had lain in the mud at the bottom of the pond.

"We need to find out who the ghost in the pond is," Charity said.

"Perhaps Claudius will tell me." Mercy began to walk to the stairs.

"Do you know where the room is?" Charity asked.

"I'll try and find it. Everything looked slightly different in the other place, because of the light. On the south side, I think, on the second floor. The next one up."

They had no light but both girls had uncanny night vision. Mercy walked ahead, trying to imagine the path she had taken through the house, behind the woman in the red silk dress. Shutting her eyes, she found she could see just as well – as though the house were a maze imprinted on her brain.

"Here," she said.

The banister was smooth and cool beneath her hand. Charity hurried to keep up. The stairs opened up on a large landing, with a tall window overlooking the conservatory, the garden with its stone lions, and Distillery Meadow beyond.

"It's cold up here." Charity shivered.

Mercy closed her eyes again, trying to remember – to feel her way to the bedroom. "This way," she said.

They walked on. Around them, the house creaked.

"I think someone's following us," Charity whispered, pulling Mercy by the elbow.

"I can't hear anyone." Something tickled her nose. The perfume, surely? "Can you smell it?" she said. "Can you smell it?"

63

"Smell what? I can't smell anything – except old carpets." Charity was still looking over her shoulder.

"Here," Mercy said. The door was locked. She took out the largest key. The lock was stiff. For a moment it resisted, then, with an audible grating, the mechanism worked.

Mercy opened the door.

A cold breath of air brushed over them. Pale curtains lifted at the window. The girls stepped inside. Something moved on the ceiling – a dark shape. Mercy's heart missed a beat.

"Ivy," she said. "The window's open. The ivy's grown into the room – covered the ceiling."

Charity stood very close to her sister. Dead leaves littered the floor, and the bed, where blankets mouldered. "Is this her room?"

"I think so."

"There aren't any pictures."

"No. But we have these." Mercy lifted the smaller keys. She walked to the dressing table and sat upon the little stool beside it. Fallen leaves lay on the glass pots. A three-panelled mirror reflected her darkly. She imagined her mother sitting in the same place, just so. Brushing her hair, fastening a necklace. Had she and Charity come here to play in the mornings? Had she climbed into the bed, and cuddled up to her mother? The room held so many memories, all locked away. Mercy strained to remember, and she couldn't. She sighed, a painful vacancy in her heart.

Charity wandered slowly around the room, touching

things. A vase by the window, the shreds of curtains. A dish full of dust, and pearls from a broken necklace. Mercy unlocked the drawer.

"Charity," she called softly. "Look." The drawer was full of letters and papers. "Give me your shawl," she said.

Charity spread out the shawl and Mercy piled it with letters. She tied up the corners.

Charity stared out of the window, into the night. "Do you really think this is our mother's room?" she said dreamily. "Did she lie here?" She dropped down on the bed, among the leaves. She curled up. "Did I lie here before, with Mother?"

"We must go," Mercy said. "We'll find her. I'm sure we will. I want to see her again too. I don't think she's dead. I think they lied to us, Charity."

They ran back to the landing, and down the stairs, helter-skelter, all the way back to Mercy's bedroom. She hid the bundle of letters under the floorboard, beneath her bed.

"Somebody was following us," Charity said. "I heard foot-steps."

Mercy nodded. "I know," she said. "I heard them too."

IV

Mercy peered down the corridor then locked her bedroom door. A grey wintery dawn was already lifting above the trees but Mercy drew her curtains and lit a candle, so they could look at the letters. It occurred to her that she had never questioned why they fell asleep at dawn – it was simply another part of the hypnotised ritual of the day. Was it possible to resist? Could they stay up and see the sun rise? Some kind of enchantment lay over the household, a repeated pattern depriving them of daylight. Perhaps they could fight it.

"Charity, do you think we could keep awake? It's not long till daylight, is it? What if we force ourselves to stay awake?" she said.

But Charity was already yawning. She looked up at her sister. "We could try," she said, doubtfully. "But I'm already so tired."

She was sitting on Mercy's bed and spilling the letters from the shawl onto the covers. The girls picked them up eagerly, one after another.

"They're written in Italian," Mercy said.

"This one's in Latin." Charity lifted the paper, trying to read the faded ink. "It's too hard for me."

"The writing's very strange," Mercy said, picking up another. The paper she held was soft, like cloth, tawny in colour and brown at the edges.

"Look," she said. Among the pile of letters, was a distinct bundle, perhaps a dozen, tied together with a piece of dusty pink satin.

"Love letters," Charity grinned. "Who are they to, and from?"

Mercy untied the ribbon and unfolded the first. "It's hard to make out the writing. They're in Italian." Mercy screwed up her eyes, trying to unravel the lines and curls. She lifted the candle, holding it close to the paper.

"Careful it doesn't burn," Charity chided.

Mercy lowered the paper, and put the candle back upon the bedside table. She looked at her sister.

"What is it?"

Mercy began slowly. "It seems, as far as I can make out, that they were addressed to Thecla, and written by Trajan. Letters from our father to our mother. The date is 1689."

They stared at each other for a moment, thoughts galloping.

"So it was certainly Thecla I saw, because these are her letters. And that must have been her room," Mercy said.

"What year is it now?"

68

"I don't know. Isn't that odd? I have a feeling 1689 was a long time ago."

"Perhaps this Trajan and Thecla are ancestors of our parents, with the same names," Charity said, grasping at straws.

"Perhaps."

They sorted the letters into piles. The bundle of old love letters in one, the other Italian letters in a second, and the Latin letters in a third. At a glance, the Italian letters were written by relatives in the old country, to Thecla and Trajan in England. Most were dated in the 1780s. Oddly, Mercy thought, the Latin letters were written at about the same time. They were addressed to Thecla, but Mercy didn't recognise the name at the bottom.

When she looked up she saw Charity was falling asleep, her head slumped on the pillow. Mercy herself was struggling to stay awake. She shook her sister.

"You must try and fight it," she said. "See if you can. Don't fall asleep."

But Charity shook her head and pushed Mercy's hand away. "Can't," she said. "Too hard."

Yawning, she stumbled to her feet and struggled to her own room next door.

Resisting her own fatigue, Mercy piled the letters back into the space beneath the floorboard, under her bed. She sat up at the desk, determined to fight the cloak of sleep. But it was hopeless. Sleep beat her down and swallowed her up. She had no choice and no effort of will would keep it away.

*

Aurelia woke her, in the darkness of Century's perverse morning. She drew the curtains, so the moonlight fell upon Mercy as she lay slumped over the desk, still dressed.

Aurelia carried a tray and placed a cup and saucer upon the table, with tea and a biscuit.

"Why aren't you in bed?" Aurelia scrutinised Mercy. "That woman's working you too hard. Neither you nor Charity is very strong."

"I am tired," Mercy agreed. She stood up from her desk and dropped onto the bed, her black hair tumbling over her shoulders. She took a biscuit, and bit it thoughtfully, staring through the window.

"Aurelia," she said slowly. "Why don't we see the daylight? Why can't I stay awake? Can you stay awake?"

Aurelia drew a breath, with a sound like a snort. "Because that's how we live."

"Why? I'm sure we used to. I remember, I think. And what year is it?"

"So many questions," Aurelia said. "What does it matter? Every day should be the same."

"Why can't I wake in the day?" she pressed. Did she want to? She remembered the hard, painful bolt of light in the other place. Sunlight could be unkind. Perhaps it was best not to see too much.

"You must speak to your father about that," Aurelia said. She touched her hair, and sighed. Then she took the tray into the next room, to wake Charity.

Mercy finished her biscuit quickly, and jumped out of bed to look at the letters again. The ancient love letters were too hard to read, so she curled up back under the covers and focused on the Latin ones instead. They were difficult to translate. The letters didn't read like her primer texts and poetry. Gradually, she began to make sense of them.

"... *of course the family understands your problem. Claudius cannot be allowed to follow his own wishes in this matter ... We live in more rational times, but the danger is still there. We can not let down our guard ...*"

She couldn't make out the next sentence. Something about the family. He had written 'Verga' and matters relating to history, and to secrecy.

The letter concluded with best wishes and love to the family – she and Charity were mentioned. The writer was one Augustus Verga. A relative, she presumed, still living, at the time, in Italy. It was dated August 1789. Mercy felt suddenly cold inside. What year was it now? She pulled the blankets higher.

The next letter was written two months later. The writer was growing angry. Whatever the problem had been, it was clearly not being resolved as he had hoped. The letter demanded action and obedience. Claudius was to be dispatched to Rome, without delay. The letter mentioned a woman several times, but she was never named.

Quickly, Mercy picked up the third letter. The tale continued. The writer's tone had changed. He wasn't angry

71

any longer. Instead the letter was a plan of action – he proposed to come to England himself in the spring to seek Claudius out. To talk with him. The woman clearly posed a greater threat than he had first supposed. And he gave her a name this time – Marietta.

Mercy's fingers, holding the letter, tingled when she read the name. She was suddenly aware of the tickle of her hair against her face, the weight of the bedclothes, the silence of the house.

Marietta.

She couldn't remember a Marietta. So why did the name have such resonance? The pages of her memory turned and turned again. But she could not put her finger to the right page.

Marietta. And someone else too.

With a brisk knock, Galatea marched into the room. Mercy stuffed the letters under the pillow.

"Mercy, time to dress. Hurry up," she said. "What are you doing?"

"I was – I was writing in my journal. I'm sorry." She scrabbled out of bed, pulling the covers back up, hoping the intruder wouldn't look.

Galatea did look. She glanced at the bed, but she didn't investigate further. She clicked her tongue and shook her head.

At breakfast Charity was lively enough, chatting with Aurelia. They ate boiled eggs and toast, served on blue-and-white china, sitting around the kitchen table. The room was warm, and for a brief moment, Mercy could believe things were as they had always been.

Once again, Galatea was busy with Trajan, and the girls were allowed time off their school work. Aurelia, doubtless following orders from their father, allowed them no opportunity to eavesdrop. She enrolled them in the bread-making, and then, while the dough proved, cast them outside for fresh air and exercise, with a stern command not to stray from the garden.

Outside, in the frosty garden, Mercy explained to Charity what she had read.

"So Claudius did something bad?" Charity wondered. "I don't really understand what it could mean. And who was Marietta?"

"I don't know what to think about Claudius at all," Mercy said. "The letters have just confused me."

But the girls didn't have long to talk. Within minutes, Galatea came hurrying out of the house, chasing after them.

In the kitchen Aurelia was kneading the dough again, her back presented to Galatea and a sour expression on her face. Mercy assumed the two women had disagreed about the care of the girls and that Aurelia wasn't supposed to have let them outside on their own, even in the garden. Aurelia had a softer heart than Galatea, but both servants were obliged to follow Trajan's orders. Mercy took off her boots.

Galatea didn't speak at first. She just stared at Mercy, her

73

face tight with anger. Mercy couldn't bear to return the stare. Obviously she had been discovered. What would her father say now? She choked on her misery, holding back tears.

"Mercy, you are a wicked girl," Galatea said. "I don't know what to say. You must go to the library and speak with your father. It is a very serious matter. Charity will stay here with Aurelia."

Mercy plodded to the library. Did they know about the theft of the letters? She dreaded the interview. Why had he picked on her, when Charity had been her willing accomplice? It was a short walk, but she took her time. She couldn't face her father. Finally standing outside the door, her heart in her mouth, she took a deep breath and knocked.

"Come in." The voice was muffled. Mercy opened the door and stepped inside. The fire was burning in the hearth. The light flickered on the backs of the books on the shelves, upon rows of Trajan's volumes concerning plants, once an obsession for him. Mercy recalled him poring over diagrams of flowers and treatises describing the new and exotic plants discovered in the New World.

The clock tinkled on the mantelpiece, chiming a quarter hour. Trajan was standing with his back to his daughter on the other side of the room, close to the shelf where she had emerged in the other, sunnier, Century. Mercy hesitated a few moments, before speaking.

"Father," she said. "Galatea told me you wished to see me."

Trajan turned around and walked across the room towards

her. She thought he was angry, but he reached out a hand and patted her shoulder.

"You look as though you've seen a ghost," he said. He smiled. "But of course, you do see ghosts."

In his other hand, Trajan was carrying a small leather bag. Mercy tried to relax. She unclasped her hands, and let them hang at her sides.

Trajan lifted the bag, snapped open the clasp at the top, and gently emptied the contents onto the table. Mercy watched in horror as her secret stash of letters tumbled one upon another onto the green table-cloth. Her mouth dropped open. She looked up at Trajan. The very last letter, on the top of the pile, was different from the others. The paper was new and fresh, and the handwriting upon it was her own – it was the letter she had written for Claudius and left at the boathouse.

Mercy shut her mouth, and opened it again. Trajan pulled out a chair for her and signalled she should sit.

"Are you angry with me?" she said, in a small voice.

Trajan sat next to her. He placed his palms flat on the table. He looked calm now.

"No," he said. "But you must tell me everything you know. We are all in great danger. The family. Matters have slipped out of my control. Galatea and Aurelia have been vigilant but Claudius is more cunning than I had suspected."

"Claudius?" Mercy blurted. Then: "Did you follow us, last night? Is that how you knew we had taken the letters?"

"Galatea followed you, Mercy. I asked her to watch you.

She has served me faithfully. Now tell me everything you know about Claudius."

Mercy bit her lip. "He said we could be free. That I could see the sun," she said. Her feelings were getting the better of her. Unexpected tears were brimming. She swallowed hard.

Trajan looked at her, and sighed. He reached out his hand and touched her cheek. The affection in the gesture was at once so pleasant and so unexpected, Mercy began properly to cry.

"We are never free of who we are," he said gently. "I know it is hard."

"What does that mean? Who are we? Who is Claudius? Why do we only wake at night?" The tears spilled. Mercy dropped her face upon her arms, on the table, and sobbed. Trajan leaned over and stroked her hair.

"There," he said. "Don't cry, Mercy. We shall be as we were, before Claudius appeared. I will keep you safe." He pulled a large handkerchief from his pocket. She lifted her head, sniffing, and he dabbed her eyes tenderly.

Mercy's heart swelled. She imagined running into Trajan's arms. Had he once picked her up and carried her? Had they played together? He seemed at once so gentle and powerful. And broken too. A man in pieces, with the centre missing. In a fit of compassion, Mercy told him about the meeting in the church, and later, in the boathouse. She told him what Claudius had said, about the ghost in the pond, and the keys to their mother's bedroom.

"You read the letters of course," he said.

"Some of them."

"And what do you deduce, from all you have learned?"

"Something happened – to do with Claudius, and now we hide in the house."

"Like Sleeping Beauty," Trajan said. "You are right, of course. The house was sealed off to protect us. To protect the family. Claudius wants to tear away our defences. But don't think he has your wellbeing at heart, Mercy. He wants to escape and destroy us. He holds us responsible for his own plight, and he wants revenge, though he's the one who brought us to this situation. Your life here – shut away – is his fault."

"How are we hidden? Where is my mother?" Mercy said. "Is it truly an enchantment? Why do we have to hide?"

But he wouldn't answer. He brushed her questions aside.

"We are different from other people," he said. "I will not tell you more, Mercy. It isn't safe for you to know. That is all I can say. Please trust me. Now go back to Galatea. Be sure to look repentant. And don't speak to Claudius, or attempt to communicate with him. If he appears again, you must tell me. I must find some way of blocking his path before he takes this any further. Then our peace will be restored."

Mercy opened her mouth to ask again, but Trajan raised his hand to silence her.

Still sniffing, Mercy rose to her feet and left the room, clutching her father's handkerchief. She didn't know what to think. How he frustrated her. She wanted – what? She wanted to know the truth about her mother. She remembered the sunlit house with a shiver of delight. Did she still want to go back?

Later, they dined with Trajan by candlelight. Then Galatea read to them in the nursery parlour until dawn. She gave the girls no opportunity to speak together, banishing them to their separate rooms when they were too tired to argue.

Mercy lay in bed with Trajan's handkerchief under her pillow. After these last troubled days, she felt a sense of relief. She could rely on her father to take care of her. Perhaps if she did as he said, the changes would cease and the pain of remembering would fade away.

After sunset, the little girl screamed; the ghost who played hide-and-seek.

Mercy woke, in a sweat, from a dream about the woman under the ice. The dream was painted in bright colours, day-time colours. In the dream Mercy ran across the meadow carrying an axe, and she buried the head deep in the frozen surface of the pond, shattering huge, glassy fragments. But the pond was hard as iron, right to the core.

The girl screamed again. Mercy jumped out of bed and ran out into the corridor. Now was her chance to slip through the door to the other place again.

No. No! She would ignore the ghost. She should go back to sleep. Her father's voice echoed in her head. His comfort.

The ghost headed for the tapestry, showing a way to the sunshine and the happy little sisters. Mercy started forward, then held back again. She was torn in two ways. The dark and the light. The cold and the heat. Comfortable familiarity – and painful change.

Trajan had been so kind. She didn't want to upset him again. Surely he knew better than she did. Then why did the other place still attract her so much? The sunlight lured, and the woman, who was her mother.

Would he know if she visited one last time, to see her? It was too much to resist. Rebellion wrestled with guilt. Mercy followed the ghost.

She closed her eyes, slipped her hand behind the tapestry and stepped into empty space. This time she was prepared for the falling sensation, but the shock of the cold plummet into space wasn't any less.

When she landed she had her fingers pressed to her eyes, against the sting of daylight. She could feel it on the backs of her hands, and her forehead. When she peeped through her fingers she saw, on the floor, Trajan's red book. Mercy stooped and picked it up, opened the cover, to see the frontispiece, the house, and the horseman. The book thrummed, charged with peculiar potency.

But she knew she couldn't take it with her so she left the book in the library and hurried along the corridor. As she passed the nursery parlour, Thecla stepped out, like the first time, with her long, golden hair, and the trail of perfume.

Mercy's heart seemed to swell when she saw her. Had she arrived at the same moment as before? Maybe Thecla would ascend to her room and hunt in the drawer again.

In the parlour the two girls were drinking tea from the cups with blue roses.

"Are you cold?" little Mercy asked her sister.

"No, not at all. In fact I am rather hot."

"I felt a chill," said the first one, with a shiver. Mercy stepped closer. Perhaps her second self had detected her presence in some way.

Mercy left the girls and wandered round the house. The wooden floors shone. The rugs were fresh and bright. She passed a servant dusting a bronze statue on a plinth, and crossed swords on a wall. Flowers bloomed in vases, filling the soft, warm air with scent. Polish, blossoms, the summer heat – she breathed it all in.

The scene shifted. Now evening was approaching, the light diffuse. The front doors were open, leading to steps. Mercy stepped tentatively outside.

The sky was a furnace of red and gold, just after sunset. How beautiful it was. Mercy shaded her eyes and stared.

She followed the sound of voices, to the orchard. The grass was long and soft. Little apples, pears, and plums fattened on the trees. She walked away from fruit trees, past the hothouses, where butterfly wings flickered behind the glass, to the rose garden.

There – the source of the sound – about a dozen children

playing on the grass, and a table, laden with dishes, beneath a canopy.

Swallows swooped over the top of the house, in a band, and skimmed the ground. Mercy watched them rise up again, and circle back over the house. The sound of their cries plucked the strings of her memory, bringing back an emotion connected with summer, with sunlight stretching deeper and deeper into the night, the warmth of the air, the perfume of grass and flowers. The emotion became a strange kind of ache, just under her ribs.

One of the children ran towards her. The girl was about nine or ten, in a long, blue dress. She skipped past Mercy, shouted out something to the others, and ran on again. Two other girls followed her. None gave any indication they had seen Mercy, shrinking against the wall, so she stepped out, to join the party on the grass.

Five girls in white dresses, like apple blossoms, sitting on a burgundy rug in the shade of rose bushes. Thecla was sitting on a chair beneath the white canopy. She was dressed in green velvet now, with her dark blonde hair coiled, and pinned up. The dress was low at the front, revealing an expanse of white skin.

What edible delights Thecla had ordered from the kitchen, for the picnic. Crystallised flowers, arranged on a silver plate – real blossoms, pink and blue and white, in a crisp sugar case. Miniature castles of cake, fish-shaped pastries, transparent sugar sweets set like gems in crowns of meringue. The children were marvelling at the feast, stuffing their moist little mouths with the trove of edible treasures.

She stared at Thecla. Although she believed the blonde woman was her mother, still something was missing. She didn't feel for her. An emotion had stirred for the summer evening, but for Thecla, nothing at all, beyond a simple curiosity. Still, Mercy couldn't stop gazing, eating up the shape of Thecla's face, the curl of her lips, the shades of wheat and honey in her hair, the pearls hanging from her ears. She edged closer, trying to breathe her mother's scent again.

"Mercy," Thecla said, in a loud, clear, voice. "Mercy, come here."

Mercy froze in an instant of terror – until she realised Thecla wasn't looking at her. Instead, a little girl on the rug turned her head around.

"Mother?" she said.

Thecla patted the chair beside her. "Come and talk to me," she coaxed.

Little Mercy sighed. She had been engrossed in a conversation with a friend, but she stood up obediently and went to her mother. The friend leaned over to watch. She had rusty auburn hair, in tight curls, a face so very familiar to Mercy. She was the ghost from the corridor outside her bedroom, who played, and sometimes screamed. Mercy put her hand to her mouth, feeling words welling up behind her lips.

Little Mercy, about ten years old, sat on the chair beside her mother and swung her legs. She picked up a sugary rose from the platter and popped it in her mouth.

"Sit still," Thecla said. "You're growing up now." Her voice was stern but she was smiling. "Are you enjoying your birthday? Are you happy?" she asked.

Little Mercy nodded. "Very happy."

"Go and play with your friends then."

Little Mercy stood up, threw her arms around her mother's neck, and kissed her on the cheek. Then she ran back to the auburn-haired girl on the rug.

Mercy moved closer still. Did she, too, want to kiss this woman, her mother? A few tiny crystals of sugar from little Mercy's lips still clung to Thecla's skin. Thecla sighed.

Mercy left the canopy and sat down on the grass, intrigued by the party of children. The three young adventurers who had run around the house returned, and plopped, out of breath, upon the grass. Eleven of them altogether, three boys and eight girls. Mercy spied little Charity at the edge of the party, spinning out a daisy chain until she started arguing with her companion, ripped up the chain, and started to sulk. When the boys had eaten their food they got up, leaped over the ha-ha, and ran down towards the lake. Mercy eavesdropped, the ghost at her own birthday party.

"Shall we walk too?" little Mercy said. "I can show you the temple. Perhaps we shall be taken in a boat on the lake." She jumped to her feet.

"Mother," she said. "Can we follow the boys? Chloe wants

to take a boat on the lake. Will you ask one of the servants to take us out?"

Chloe. Chloe. Yes, she remembered. Her best and dearest friend. Mercy froze, her eyes fixed on the little girl. How had she forgotten? So many chambers in her heart had been locked up. No wonder she always felt cold. But, yes, she remembered now. Chloe had loved her despite her shyness and awkward manners and odd fierce outbursts. Chloe had understood exactly what little Mercy meant to say and why she laughed, and understood too the realms of her imagination. Mercy stared at the little girl and felt the emptiness of the lost time that divided them.

Thecla stood up, and brushed off her skirts.

"Come along," she said. "Children, are you ready?" She nodded to a white-wigged footman, standing discreetly beside the canopy, and he followed the party along the gravel pathway to the garden gate. Encumbered by skirts, the girls were unable to jump the ha-ha.

Sheep were grazing in the field leading down to the lake. Shorn, they looked diminished, like goats. They bounded away when the party approached. The ground was dotted with droppings.

Mercy wondered where the other adults were – probably in the house, enjoying their own entertainments. Thecla had taken it upon herself to care for the younger members of the party. Mercy was tempted to run back to the house to find out what was happening, and who the other visitors might be.

However, the twilight was beautiful – she didn't want to miss a minute.

The footman took Chloe and little Mercy to the boathouse, now freshly-painted, and pristine. In fact, the house and the grounds possessed the same crisp, raw air of something newly-finished, and not yet settled into the surrounding countryside. Of course, the Verga family had commissioned the building of the house, the gardens and grounds. How long had they lived here at this time?

The girls skipped down the wooden steps into the boat. Mercy stepped in cautiously beside them. Mercy sat at the prow, squeezed in. Then the footman climbed down and took up the oars.

"Who's taken the other boat?" little Mercy said.

"The boys," Chloe said. "Can't you hear them?"

As their own vessel moved out of the darkening boathouse, Mercy saw three boys in a little rowing boat splashing ineffectively with the oars. The ducks quacked in alarm, and scattered into the rushes nearby.

"No," little Mercy said. "There's a third one. The prettiest boat, with a canopy. Someone else must have taken it."

The surface of the lake was very still and midnight blue, with ripples of cobalt and bars of gold where the water reflected the last glowing shots of sunlight on the clouds.

"Don't be long," Thecla called. "It'll be dark soon."

"Take us to the island," little Mercy commanded. "Chloe wants to see the temple."

The footman expertly turned the boat. The lake was shaped like a giant's footprint, in long curves. The island rose in the middle, visible from Century, a focal point in the grand design. From outside the house, the artfully ruined temple looked grand and imposing. Close up, Mercy remembered, it was less impressive.

It only took a few minutes to reach the island. The footman brought the boat to rest at a tiny pier on the lee side, where the third, larger boat was already moored. The girls clambered out. Mercy hurried after them. She had a feeling she already knew who had brought the third boat to the tiny island. Chloe and little Mercy were laughing, walking side by side, heads close together as if they were sharing a secret. They talked nineteen to the dozen. The island was no natural feature, of course. Like the nearby river cascade, and the grotto, it was an artifice, just large enough to carry the carefully ruined temple and half a dozen trees. As the girls drew nearer, they began to whisper, hiding their mouths behind their hands. They tiptoed. Now Mercy could hear a male voice, coming from the temple, confirming her suspicions. Little Mercy and Chloe climbed the earth bank behind it. They lay down upon their stomachs, peeping over the top, down to the people below. Mercy followed suit.

"It's your sister," little Mercy whispered to Chloe. They were lying shoulder to shoulder.

Among the fluted marble columns and the tumbled blocks, beneath the roof still large enough to provide shelter and shade for the visitors, a romantic scene unfolded. Rugs and cushions, and a basket of food. Claudius partly reclined, and a young woman lay with her head upon his shoulder. They weren't speaking, but Claudius stroked her hand, and then her cheek. He must have heard the girls because he looked around.

"They've sent spies," he said. "We're not alone, Marietta."

The woman laughed, and sat up straight, rearranging her dress.

"Come along Mercy, and Chloe," Claudius said loudly. "It isn't any use hiding. We saw the boat coming across the lake. And we could hear you whispering."

He was good-humoured, teasing them. He stood up. "Shall I come and find you?" he said. "You force my hand. Come! If you reveal yourselves now, we might share this delicious damson and honey pudding. Otherwise I might eat it all myself."

The girls looked at each other – made some unspoken agreement – then clambered to their feet and ran back down the bank to the temple. Mercy followed them, slowly. She was afraid Claudius would see her, so she remained outside the temple, obscured by the wall.

From this unsatisfactory vantage point she studied Marietta as best she could. Like Chloe, she had very fair skin and auburn hair, though Marietta's was darker, more like claret, and straight, while Chloe's curled. She was very slender, with long, elegant hands.

She was the ghost under the ice.

Of course. Of course!

Everything was known. The difficulty lay in the remembering.

Mercy squeezed her hands into tight fists. She looked again at Marietta, remembering the covering of ice, like a veil, and the drowned-green colour of Marietta's hair under the water.

The company was happy. Marietta sliced the pudding and teased her little sister. Little Mercy was sitting on a marble step beside Claudius.

"How is the birthday girl?" he asked. "Have you enjoyed your party?"

"Yes, thank you," little Mercy said, cuddling Claudius's arm.

"And Chloe, did you eat plenty of cake?"

Chloe nodded. "Lots," she said.

"Well, here we all are," Claudius said. "Isn't this pleasant? And I have a gift for you, Mercy. It's in the basket. Look."

Little Mercy lifted out a cloth from the bottom of the basket. She drew out a small velvet box. It was red, patterned with gold stitching.

"Open it," Chloe urged. Claudius nodded. Slowly, little Mercy raised the lid. Resting inside, she found two pearls, shaped like tears, on gold wires. She didn't speak. She stared.

"Do you like them?" Marietta asked gently. Still little Mercy didn't speak. She lifted her eyes to Claudius, her lips parted.

"Earrings," Chloe said. "They are so beautiful. Real pearls. You are so lucky. May I try them on?"

Little Mercy shook her head. She closed the lid, and held the box tight.

"It's getting rather dark," Marietta said. "We'd better return to the house." She began to tidy away the meal and the blankets.

"Go back with the girls," Claudius said. "I want to stay here on my own for a moment. I like the dark."

Marietta looked displeased. "I want to be with you," she said.

"Please?" he said. "I won't be long. I have a lantern for the boat."

Marietta hesitated for a moment, then agreed. Claudius carried the basket back to the boat, where the footman waited patiently. Marietta, Chloe and little Mercy climbed aboard, and the boat pulled away from the island. They waved at Claudius as they departed.

When the boat was halfway back to the shore, Claudius returned to the temple.

He sat upon the topmost of the five steps. Mercy sat beside him. The last glimmers of colour had disappeared from the blackening surface of the lake. In front of them, Century loomed at the top of the hill. On the far shore, by the water's edge, the children were following Thecla towards the house. Behind the island, the woodland at the lake's perimeter had filled with darkness. A light wind blew off the lake, into their faces. Far away, among the trees, the chorus of robins ceased their sad, reedy song, leaving only the long, wistful notes of the nightingale, who would sing for the rest of the night. Honeysuckle and dog roses grew over one of the white columns.

"This was the most perfect day of my life," Claudius said. "Nothing before, and nothing after, could ever match it." He turned to Mercy. "My heart was full," he said. "Complete – the time I was most myself. The day I wanted to last for ever. And now it does."

V

Mercy hugged her legs and stared out across the lake.

"What year is it?" she said.

"A good question," Claudius replied. "Now? Or where you came from?"

"Both."

"This is the summer of 1789. You know the date, of course," he said.

"My birthday." She frowned, struggling to remember. "June the first? Now tell me the year of the other place, where I have come from."

Claudius regarded her. "It is 1890," he said. "Just over a hundred years have passed."

Mercy pressed her nails into the palms of her hands. She didn't believe him. But she remembered the letters, the curious dates from long, long ago.

"How can that be true?" she demanded. "That means I'm over a hundred years old, and so are you. That's impossible."

Claudius sighed. "Trajan has never told you about the family," he said.

"The family," she said. "What about it? We come from Italy, I know. The old country."

"The Vergas are not like other people," he said. "We live for hundreds of years, Mercy. As far as I can tell, we live for ever. We grow to adulthood, and then remain as we are. Of course if I met an accident I would die – if I was murdered, if I cast myself from a steeple top. Otherwise – no death. Death isn't natural for us."

Mercy's head buzzed. Could it be true?

"But Trajan looks old now," she said. "And why am I still a child after one hundred years? Nothing you tell me makes sense."

"As adults, our outward appearance reflects the condition of our hearts," Claudius explained. "You father is old because he has lost the desire to live. If he underwent a change of heart, Trajan would become young again. Grief makes us old. Happiness brings youth. And as for you Mercy – you haven't grown up because, as you are beginning to understand for yourself, Trajan has caught you in a deep enchantment. He has hidden you away and caught you up in one little piece of time, played over and over again." He stopped and looked at her carefully.

"You look very thin and tired," he said. "The winter weather doesn't suit you."

"How is it that you can see me, and the others can't?"

"They are puppets in a show, rehearsing their parts. Their

minds don't register your presence. They are the past and you aren't a part of their time – their chapter in the story."

"What about you?"

"I have broken out of the story. I brought you here. I'm not playing the game any more."

"Why? Father says you want to destroy the house."

Claudius didn't answer for a few moments. Then he took a deep breath. "Tell me about your day, Mercy," he said. "Before you saw the ghost in the pond, and everything started to come undone."

"The night," she said. "Cold wintertime. Frost in the garden, a walk outside. Aurelia in the kitchen, lessons with Galatea. Stories with Charity in the nursery parlour."

"Do you know how long that night has taken?"

"You have led me to believe it's been a hundred years," she said.

"You've been buried alive. You can't remember how old you are, or how long you've lived in the house. They have shut you away from the daylight, from life itself. You exist, merely. You have no sense of the story of the past, nor anticipation for the future. I want you to have these things, Mercy. Does that sound like destruction?"

"Why should Father lie to me?" she said. "Doesn't he want what's best for us?"

"Your father is afraid. He hasn't the courage to live any more."

Mercy sighed. Such a relief to receive answers at last – like water quenching a thirst – even answers from Claudius, her father's enemy. Perhaps it was disloyal to listen to the version of events Claudius laid before her – but Trajan wouldn't tell her anything. What else could she do?

She frowned. "But it was you," she said. "It was you and Marietta who brought us to this. Isn't that right?"

"Yes," Claudius said. His voice was very level. "This – situation – is a consequence of your parents' reaction to my marriage to Marietta."

"Where is Thecla now – in my time?"

"You can find her."

"Is she – is she still alive?" Hope stirred, a fluttering in her chest.

Claudius shook his head. It was a curious response. Did he mean yes – or no?

"Why won't you give me a straight answer?" she said angrily. "Where is my mother?"

"First you have to seek her out," Claudius said. "And before that, you have to find the key to unlock the cage – the tyranny of days."

"The day you wanted to last for ever," Mercy said.

"Yes. But now I want that day to end too." Claudius pushed back the hair from his face. For a moment the nightingale was silent. Then it began to sing again; long, throbbing notes. "It was a perfect moment," he said. "How we want to seize them and hold them tight. But we have to let them go – to kiss the joy as it flies – because without change we may as well be dead and buried."

Mercy breathed the scent of the honeysuckle, and the roses.

"How did you break out, to find me?" she said. "Why now, after so long?"

"My marriage ended in death and loss," Claudius said. "It has taken me this long to reconcile myself to the events of the past."

Mercy remembered the ghost under the ice, and Marietta's drowned face.

"How did it happen?" she said. "Why did Marietta die?"

But Claudius ignored her questions. He ploughed on. "For so many years I've relived the events of the past, until the feelings wore out and passed away. Even this day became empty in the end – the emotion grown thin. I allowed Trajan to lock me up – and now I want to break out."

"And you want me to help you?" Mercy said. "Why should I do that? My father won't tell me what happened, but you give me only fragments. You don't answer all my questions either."

"If you help me, you will find your mother, and you'll restore Century to life," Claudius said. "Isn't that what you want?"

Mercy bunched her hands into fists. "What do I have to do?" she said.

"Trajan's spell is a story," Claudius said. "We are, each of us, trapped in different chapters of the tale."

"A story," Mercy repeated. She remembered the red book in the library with her father's name in it. The book that seemed to hum in her hands.

"Trajan is one of the most remarkable of the Verga family and he has great talents," Claudius said. "He didn't want his ability. He ran away from the gift he was given – resolved never to use it. I think he was afraid of it."

"A great talent," Mercy said, wonderingly. "A supernatural gift? The power to cover the house in darkness – is that what you're saying? Why did he do it?"

"At the very beginning of 1790, Century witnessed such a tragedy that Trajan decided to use his gift because he thought it would protect us – the family."

"He wrote the book," Mercy interrupted. "The book called *Century*. That's how he did it."

Claudus nodded. "He broke up the past and locked each piece in a separate place, to keep it safe. To preserve it. He pulled a cloak over the house, so people should walk past without seeing it – just as the people here don't see you.

"Outside, the house has continued to exist, and now stands the year of Our Lord 1890 – a miraculous world of inventions you could not dream of. Inside the house, we're bottled up in one of five single days."

Mercy hugged her legs. It was too much to take in at once.

"Do you want to end it, Mercy?" he asked gently.

She nodded.

"You are in the outermost space," he said. "Imagine the five days are held in globes, one inside the other, like a Russian doll. Your day is like the big doll on the outside. Your Century is closest to the ordinary world. Time hasn't entirely stopped in the region you inhabit. You are a little older than the Mercy you saw on her birthday today. Trajan needed the first place to be a buffer against the outside world – just in case anyone should break through. A place to link the past and the present."

"Yes." Mercy frowned. "Then why is it always dark? I don't think the sun ever shines on Century now. Nothing grows."

"No," Claudius said. "Trajan used the darkness like a veil to hide the house. A passer-by in 1890 wouldn't notice the house at all. It is there, of course. But someone outside wouldn't see it. Their eyes would slide over. They wouldn't notice it."

"So I have stepped in – to this, the second space?"

Claudius nodded.

"Visit them all, Mercy," he said. "Remember everything. Join the story together again. You have to write the story anew. Resolve the puzzle. Then we shall be free."

He reached inside his coat and drew out a folded paper, and a book, bound in red leather. He opened the paper.

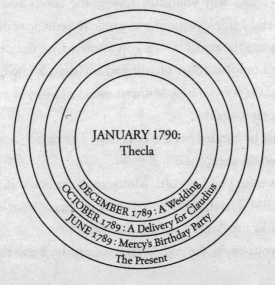

JANUARY 1790:
Thecla

DECEMBER 1789: A Wedding

OCTOBER 1789: A Delivery for Claudius

JUNE 1789: Mercy's Birthday Party

The Present

"Look," he said. "See how the five days nestle one inside another."

Mercy took the paper and stared.

"There are doorways from one day to the next," Claudius said. "I discovered them, one by one. I learned where they could be found. I used one of the doors, by the tapestry, to come and visit you. Once, I used the others to reach the centre. There I picked a snowdrop and I brought it back to you.

"But I don't find it easy to move from one place to another. Trajan trapped me here and it takes every ounce of strength I have to slip from one place to another. It is easier for you."

"Why is it easier for me? Why do I have to write the story? Why can't you?" Mercy asked.

Claudius smiled. "Simply, because you are more powerful than me," he said. "You have inherited your father's gift, Mercy. That's why you must rewrite the book. You can see ghosts, and I think you can use words to reshape reality. And you can use the doors. Once you know where the doors are, you need only an effort of will and the right frame of mind. You've done it twice now, without even knowing how. I think you can do it again."

Finally he handed her the red book. The name *Century* was embossed on the front.

"This is for you," he said. Mercy took the book. It was just like the one Trajan had written, only the pages were blank.

"It's like my father's book," she said.

"It's your book," he said. "Write your story. Break the cage."

"Where are the doors?" she said.

"In the library, in each day, find *The Precise Geography of the Lermantas Archipelago* and tucked in the cover you'll find a map showing the location of the door into the next chapter. You will have to act swiftly, because any time you are dropped back in your own time your father will try and stop you. Do you understand?" He gripped her hard, digging his fingers into her skinny arm.

"Yes," she said, pulling away. "Yes."

Claudius shook his head. Then he clapped both hands to his temples, and screwed up his face. The nightingale's long note cut off.

Claudius momentarily lifted himself from whatever seizure had possessed him, and delivered a manic, unsettling smile. Then he disappeared.

It was the end of the chapter. No need to return to the library to find a door to her own time. The lake, the temple, the house on the hill, all folded up and blinked out. Mercy was sitting in empty space. She shot up –

– to her cold, dark home. To the corridor outside her bedroom.

How icy the air – how heavy the night. She still held the empty red book and the diagram illustrating the five days in circles, so she took them to her room, locked the door, and hid them under the floorboard beneath her bed. Then she lay down, exhausted. A fire burned in the hearth. The weight of her journey lay upon her limbs, though she struggled to sleep.

Her thoughts wandered. She looked around the familiar room. Now it also seemed strange. She noticed how dirty it was, cobwebs hanging dustily from the ceiling. Of course it hadn't changed – but she had.

Aurelia woke her, rattling the door, demanding entrance. Mercy unlocked the door to receive a tray and tea. She drew the curtains. High up, the moon curved, like the sword of a robber in her *Book of the Arabian Nights*. The dead snowdrop had been cleared away.

Mercy took off her nightgown. The bruise on her knee from her fall on the ice had almost disappeared. She unfolded her underclothes, and the pink gown, and dressed. How faded and stained it was. She hadn't noticed before. The fabric was thin and patched. The bottom of the skirt, where the hems brushed the floor, were brown with grime and worn threadbare.

She looked around the bedroom. A wardrobe stood against the far wall, a dressing table to the right. The dressing table had a winged mirror. Every evening, when she woke, Mercy sat at the table and brushed her hair. Today, she noticed a thick film of dust covered the mirror, and every item on the dressing table – except for her hairbrush. She had pink glass pots, a crystal vase, a hand mirror with an embroidered back, a perfume bottle – all covered with the soft, grey shawl of dust. She picked up a velvet box, a faded red with gold stitching. The hinges broke when she opened it. Inside, on the velvet pad, lay two pearl earrings. She lifted them out. Were her ears still pierced? Yes. She put the earrings on. She stared at her obscure reflection in the mirror. Claudius was right. She did look thin and tired. Like an old lady, she thought. I'm so worn and faded, and I've only really lived a handful of years.

She stretched out her hand and wrote her name in the dust. Mercy Galliena Verga. And the year – 1890. A spider skittered along a thread of silk, to the web spun between the mirror and the table top. She peered into the mirror, searching her face, trying to imagine how she would look if her dress was not old and soiled. How would people see her now, if they could, the ordinary people living in the light outside of the secret house? She felt very small and tired, like a thread drawn out too long and thin, now close to snapping.

Mercy carefully replaced the box and the hairbrush in their prints in the dust. She went to the wardrobe and turned the tiny key in the door. Inside hung a row of dresses, red and blue and gold, some embroidered and jewelled, like princesses waiting for a ball. They had lingered a hundred years, these tired, greying princesses, under an enchantment, destined, perhaps, to wait for ever. The passage of time had undone them. When Mercy drew out the first, on its hanger, the sleeve came away from the dress. Moth larvae had nibbled the silk. She sighed, and replaced it carefully, with its sisters.

"It's no good," she said to herself. "It can't carry on." Her fingers shook as she locked the wardrobe. She wouldn't let it continue. A spirit of rebellion flared in her chest – anger rattled in a locked up box.

Charity was sitting at the table in the old nursery parlour. She toyed with a tarnished silver egg-cup. Mercy sat at the other end of the table.

The parlour had not deteriorated as badly as her own room. It was a little dusty and untidy, the furniture showing signs of wear and tear, but it did look lived in. The fire burned in the hearth.

"Is that all you can eat?" Mercy said.

Charity shrugged.

"Well, you haven't eaten anything at all yet." Her wine-coloured dressing gown was covered in stains, unravelled and patched like Mercy's dress.

"It's funny how easy it is to fall into that same conversation, isn't it?" Mercy said.

"Yes," Charity said. "All the same, everything seems to be changing. The day isn't the same any more, is it?"

Mercy leaned forward, and whispered: "I went there again – to the place in the past. Now I know what I have to do. I know the name of the ghost in the pond."

"Who is she?"

"Marietta," Mercy whispered. "Claudius's wife. And the little-girl ghost in my corridor is her sister, Chloe – my best friend."

She had no time to speak further because Aurelia bustled in, with her tray and toast and the plates decorated with blue roses.

When they had finished eating, there was still no time to talk. Galatea joined them in the parlour. They began with Latin verbs, but unexpectedly Trajan called in and asked for Mercy to join him on a walk. Mercy coloured. Even Galatea was flustered.

Aurelia fetched Mercy's hat and coat. Trajan looked different now. He had washed and changed his clothes. Nervous with guilt, Mercy tried to measure his mood. He had reached out to her, the day before. And she had betrayed him.

He seemed more tired than angry. They walked across Distillery Meadow. Trajan pointed at the glitter of frost on the grass, and Venus rising, like a fat green cabbage in the sky. When they walked to the pond, Mercy hung back at first, afraid of what they might see. But Trajan beckoned her forward beside him. The ice was white, under a layer of frost.

They stared at the pond. Trajan brooded. Mercy grew cold. She rubbed her gloved hands together. Her cheeks tingled.

"You've seen him again," he said. "You disobeyed me."

"Seen who? I haven't seen anyone," she said quickly.

"Mercy, don't lie to me."

Mercy didn't know what to say, and she didn't know who to trust, and what to believe. She loved her father – but she remembered the smell of honeysuckle and roses, and the summer air, and the swallows. She thought of her room covered with dust, and the mouldering dresses. If Claudius was telling the truth, it was Trajan who insisted they live like this.

"I don't believe Claudius," she said. "He tells me lies. I don't listen."

She was herself a poor liar. She rubbed her face with her hands, her cheeks hot.

"Mercy," he said again. "You went to the other place."

"I didn't. I didn't!"

103

"Mercy!" He was angry now. "Do I have to beat you? Or lock you up? That is what I shall do if I have to."

Mercy bit her lip.

"He has told you, hasn't he? About the cloak over Century, about our long lives?"

Mercy nodded.

"Can't you see?" he said. "You little fool, can't you put two and two together? Every time you move from one place to another, they begin to fall apart. Just a little the first time, then a bit more, and more again – until we are entirely undone.

"This is my spell, Mercy. My cunning and power created the shape of it. And each time you step from your place into one of the others, they all start to unravel. I can feel it in my bones. Already Claudius has caused damage, with his meddling and wandering. Now you are making it worse. Finally the whole edifice will collapse and we will be exposed and vulnerable again. I want to protect you, but you are determined to help him destroy us all!"

Mercy felt tears come to her eyes. She tried to choke them back, staring at her feet.

"I didn't know," she said. But of course she had known, on some level. Time itself had undone Century. All the little changes – the dust and cobwebs, and the decay in the house, were simply the result of one hundred years of neglect. Now as the spell began to unravel she could see it truly for the first time. The veil was torn from her eyes. So what was she doing to the other days? Were they coming apart at the seams, the more she meddled, Claudius-like?

"He told me I had inherited your powers," she said, in a small voice. "Is it true?"

"I think it is, Mercy, because you have the power to see outside our own place," he said, more gently now. "Your ghosts. Do you understand? Echoes from the other times. You can see through the walls of the days."

"I want to find out what happened to my mother – where she is. And I don't want to be held here for ever!" she cried. "I want to see Thecla. I want the summer to come, and the daylight. Who would hurt us now, if a hundred years have passed? Won't the people outside have forgotten whatever happened? Why won't you tell me who we are?"

"It is more than the events of the past we need to hide from," he said. "We hide because we're different. I thought we could live as ordinary people, but I was wrong. We live for so long. It changes everything. And our difference always causes bad things to happen. We have to lock ourselves away for ever – to keep ourselves safe, to keep others safe. Because of who we are."

He turned away from the pond, and they walked back, along the giant hedgerow at the edge of the meadow. Moodily, Trajan swiped at the dead stalks and bare twigs with his black stick. Mercy didn't dare ask him another question. She walked beside him in silence back to the house, trying to swallow her sense of injustice. Outside the door, he turned to her again.

"Don't go," he said. "Remember your sister. Don't you want to protect her?"

Mercy nodded. She was too upset to speak so she stepped past him into the house, where Aurelia was baking. Trajan marched away, into the depths of the house, leaving Mercy at the kitchen table, bottling the ache of her own confusion. How could he manipulate her like that, suggesting she had put Charity in danger? She loved him so much, and now he had made her so cross and unhappy. She hugged herself tight, as though she could hold everything together, and she stared, unseeing, at the kitchen wall.

Unasked, Aurelia placed a cup of chocolate upon the table beside her.

"Thank you," Mercy said mechanically.

"I like your earrings," Aurelia said. "I haven't seen you wearing them before."

"I think I'll go to my room," Mercy said abruptly, picking up her drink. "I'm tired."

Mercy locked her bedroom door, and took her red book from its hiding place. She sat at the desk, and pulling out the little drawers, she discovered her own old letters and note-books, mouldering and hard to read. She lifted out her journal, where she had scribbled her stories and poems. This pastime had been such a consolation – but now, rereading her tales and rhymes, the words did not make any sense. She put them to one side.

Instead she found a quill, dipped it in ink, took a deep

106

breath, and opened the red book. In the front she wrote *Century: A Novel.* Then her name. Mercy Galliena Verga. And the year, 1890.

She turned to the first page, and wrote the chapter number, in a Roman numeral. This would not be another journal, but a story. Claudius had told her to write her own history of Century, a retelling of the hundred-year-long story and everything that happened in the huge old house. Only this time it would have a happy ending.

Where to start? She knew exactly where. She wrote:

A woman under the ice.

Once she had written this first sentence, Mercy stopped. She looked out the window. Did she understand what she was doing? Could she trust Claudius? Truth to tell, she didn't trust him. However, he was right about one thing. She and Charity were buried alive, and an endless existence without change could no longer be endured. Trajan had locked them all up in one long night of cold and dust and frost. Where was the kindness in that?

She bit the end of the quill. She knew what the book should look like – and it needed drawings. She would have to enrol Charity if the spell was going to work. She would have to persuade her.

The candle spilled a pool of yellow light over the bureau, the book, upon her hands and face. She only had an hour. She began to write again.

A ghost. Mercy could see ghosts . . .

107

Galatea took them for another walk after lunch. They headed down to the lake and around the water's edge. Mercy was lost in her own thoughts, thinking about her writing. Even Charity was subdued. The darkness oppressed. They were tired of the cold. The glittering frost had lost its magic. Later, Galatea went off to confer with Trajan. Aurelia stoked the fires and cooked hot fruit puddings. She was curiously lively, trying to cheer them up with chatter. Mercy wondered how old Aurelia really was. She belonged to the Verga clan, just like Claudius and Galatea, Thecla and Charity. She, if Claudius was right, would live for hundreds of years. Was Aurelia tired of the darkness too? But Mercy could not turn to Aurelia for help. However much she loved the housekeeper, Mercy knew Aurelia owed her allegiance to Trajan, that she would faithfully follow his commands. Aurelia and Galatea, unlike Mercy, would have utter faith in their master's judgement.

Mercy went to her room but when she tried to lock the door she found the key was missing. Her desk had been disturbed, with papers pushed out of place. Luckily the red book was safely in the secret place beneath her bed, under the floorboard. Mercy was annoyed but not at all surprised. Presumably Galatea or her father had checked her room. She opened the curtains and stared across the garden to the fields beyond. For a moment her energy and resolve seemed to desert her. Gazing into the darkness, she was overcome with a sense of dreariness. She didn't know what to do. The problems she faced seemed so complex, so hard to overcome. One part of her still wanted to curl up and sleep, to return to the unending revolutions of the dream she had lost – the day that never ended. But it was too late for that – she had already broken the dream into pieces. Like the princess in *Sleeping Beauty*, she had finally woken up. Claudius had battered down the hedge of thorns and found her in the tower.

She pressed her face against the cold glass. There was nothing for it. She had to go on. She had more to write – and Charity, who was a better artist than she was, had to draw the pictures. How would Charity draw Claudius? As a child she must have seen him. Could she remember him now?

Mercy shut the door and pushed a rug in front of it, to obstruct nosey visitors. She retrieved the red book from its hiding place and turned to the last words she had written. It was hard to write. She chewed the top of the quill, thinking how much more she had to find out to complete the book. The telling of the whole story required another, longer journey into the past. She dipped the pen into the ink and began to write about the summer birthday party, and the meeting with Claudius and Marietta on the island. The writing completely absorbed her attention, sucking her in.

Suddenly the door burst open, the rug flying out. Before Mercy had time to hide what she was doing, a claw gripped the back of her neck. A painful, iron grasp – like a vice. Mercy tried to pull away.

"What are you doing?" Galatea hissed. Mercy could smell

the governess's breath close to her cheek – a peculiar mixture of stale dust and peppermint.

"Hasn't your father explained, you foolish, disobedient little girl? What will it take for you to learn and understand? Are you intent on bringing ruin upon us all?"

Galatea was white with rage, features all screwed into a knot in the centre of her face. She bared her teeth. Then she pulled Mercy to her feet and dragged her out of the bedroom, along the corridor. Mercy shouted out, kicking and yelling. She dragged her feet.

"Charity, help me! Charity! Let me go!"

She fought like a demon, kicking up clouds of dust. Galatea's hard fingers encircled her wrists now, and although the governess was slight, she was irresistible.

"Charity!" Mercy called. "Father! Stop it! Let me go!"

Behind her, Mercy thought she heard a door open as she wailed. She tried to look round. Nobody stepped to her rescue and Galatea was immune to her entreaties. She dragged her up another flight of stairs, through a door in a panelled wall, and up a narrow stairway to the top floor. She pushed Mercy into a small, dark room and slammed the door shut. Mercy heard a key turn in the lock. A bolt shot home at the top of the door, another at the bottom. Outside Galatea gave a deep sigh. The sound of footsteps receded as she walked slowly down the little stairway.

Mercy sat on the bare floorboards for a few minutes, catching her breath. She wiped the tears from her eyes with her sleeve. She was appalled. How could her life have come to this? A prisoner! She wrung her hands, hot tears still leaking. What would happen now? The minutes passed. She waited, expecting Galatea to return at any moment, or her father. She couldn't believe she would be left locked up for long, even though her father had threatened it, even though she had disobeyed him. But the minutes stretched out and nobody came. Mercy kept her eyes fixed on the door, waiting for release. Five minutes, ten.

"Come on," she muttered. "Let me out. Let me out."

Then she jumped to her feet and hammered on the door with her fists.

"Help!" she shouted. "Let me out! Let me out!"

The noise echoed around the house, and still nobody came. Fired up with outrage, she tugged at the door handle and kicked the door hard, once, twice. The dull thud of her boots made little impression on the thick wood. Anger ebbed away, leaving a rising tide of hopelessness. Mercy sank to her knees and pressed her face into her hands.

Maybe an hour passed, it was hard to tell. No one was coming to her rescue. Trajan either didn't know, or didn't care. She had only her own resources to rely on. All alone, Mercy sat up and looked round the room.

She guessed it had been servants' quarters in the beginning. Two narrow beds were pressed against the wall, covered with boxes. The room was very dim, without a light, and two low, ungenerous windows let in a dusting of moonlight. The place

111

was heaped haphazardly with crates – presumably when the servants were dispatched, it had evolved into a junk room.

Mercy stood up, and uselessly tried the door again. The windows were tiny, with two metal bars across them. In any case, they were too high for escape. The door was locked with two bolts outside besides. It was the perfect prison.

Mercy pushed the boxes from the first bed and curled up on the hard straw mattress. She was very cold. The eaves let in an icy draught, and she could hear the scratching of mice in the ceiling. She tucked her hands into her sleeves and tried to keep warm. What would Galatea do with the red book? Probably she would take it straight to Trajan, and he would throw it on the fire, and Mercy would have lost her chance to escape the long, winter night. Instead, she would be trapped here for ever, unable to see the sun and the day, the wheel of the seasons.

How cold it was. She began to cry again, quiet sobs, her tears salty on her cheeks. She wanted to be warm. She wanted her mother to put her arms around her, and kiss her. She remembered the picnic on the grass, and the sight of Thecla, and the child Mercy running to be fussed and cuddled. She summoned up the memory of honeysuckle, and the nightingale. Slowly, the imaginings carried her off, and she drifted into a chilly, paralysed sleep on the uncomfortable bed.

VI

The mice rattled noisily in the rafters. Mercy dreamed she was standing in a room full of stuffed animals, where Claudius studied papers at a desk. The menagerie of stuffed animals – foxes, squirrels, a badger – would not keep still. They were trying to escape, but their feet were pinned. She heard a growl and a bleat. In the dream, Claudius lifted his face from the page he studied so intently and said: "Don't worry. I can set you free." He blinked and smiled, but Mercy was afraid because all around her the creatures were becoming frantic, tearing themselves to pieces.

"Mercy," Claudius said, in her dream. "Mercy, wake up."

Mercy opened her eyes.

"Mercy. Are you in there? Can you move?" The door rattled.

"Charity?" Mercy said. She climbed stiffly from the bed. She was so cold. Her fingers were numb. She hobbled to the door.

"Charity, is that you?"

"Yes!" Charity said.

"I think Galatea has the key in her pocket. You could steal it and let me out. You can win her round. She dotes on you."

"She doesn't trust me any more," Charity said.

"Why not?"

"Because I've taken your book." She lowered her voice. "I heard when she dragged you off, and you were screaming, so I sneaked into your room and picked up the book, and hid it. Galatea was mad when she came back and the book had gone. She threatened me with a whipping if I wouldn't tell her where it was. I swore blind I hadn't taken it. She took me to Father and I did the whole act all over again. I don't think they believed me – but they're not quite sure one way or the other." Charity drew breath. "Mercy – I can't stay," she said. "They'll wonder where I am. But don't worry – I'll think of a way to get you out of there."

"Charity – wait! Charity! I'm so cold," Mercy called out. She could hear her sister's footsteps hopping down the stairs, and once again she was trapped, on her own, in the mean little room.

She stood up and rubbed her arms. They wouldn't leave her to starve. Galatea, she presumed, would return with food before too long. Surely Trajan wouldn't allow the governess to keep her locked up in the icy room? She sat on the bed, staring for a few blank moments, and then she began to poke at the boxes and crates stacked up around the room. Perhaps one of them contained a rug or some clothing she could use to keep warm.

She rummaged in the first box, and found only household documents. It was too dark to read, but she could make out that the heavy journals were ledgers containing lists of figures. Other boxes contained rusty cutlery and tools. One, on the other bed, was stuffed with a heavy length of fabric. Mercy heaved the musty-smelling material from the box. Old curtains. They would help keep her warm – though perfumed with mouse.

She slept again, fitfully. When she woke, the key was turning in the lock. Galatea stepped into the room with a lamp, followed by Aurelia. Mercy ran to the housekeeper, and threw her arms around her waist.

"There," Aurelia said. "Poor lamb." Then, remembering herself, she reluctantly disentangled Mercy's arms. "Of course you should have behaved, young lady. It does seem terribly hard, though, shutting her up like this."

"Be quiet," Galatea snapped. "We're following the master's orders. She'll be safer in here because there's no chance of her escaping. We can make it more comfortable. It's for her own good."

They brought in proper bedding, and Galatea set the lamp on the floor. They cleared a little table, and Aurelia carried in a tray with a pork chop on a plate, under a silver cover, a pot of chocolate, and various other edibles. Galatea had even thought to bring Mercy's favourite books.

"There," Aurelia said, pushing a chamber pot under the bed. "You have everything you need for now. I'll look in with your breakfast."

Mercy nodded sadly. She knew Aurelia wouldn't disobey Trajan. She could only wait for Charity to find a way to let her out.

She slept again, and read her books. The hours stretched. She lay on the bed, thoughts drifting, trying to tease memories of the past from the dark spaces in her mind. She was losing track of time. At some point, while she slept, the chamber pot was emptied, and another tray of food appeared, though she hadn't eaten from the last one. She waited patiently for Charity, longing for her little sister to come back.

Perhaps a day passed. Mercy fell into a state of listlessness. She dreamed and dozed and dreamed again, sleep and waking becoming confused. She shouted out in her sleep and the sound of her voice woke her up, though she didn't know what she said. And often she woke crying, surfacing from lakes of loss and unhappiness in long, dark dreams to the cold comfort of the servants' room and the scuttling feet of mice.

She didn't eat. Once she woke to find Aurelia leaning over her, the governess in the background. Aurelia wiped her face with a warm flannel, concern written all over her face. Galatea stood straight as a poker in the background, a forbidding presence and, although she longed to throw her arms around the housekeeper's neck, Mercy restrained herself, holding onto her tears till the door was shut and locked again.

She didn't sleep deeply, battling with the plague of dreams. Her own mind was a maze of locked-up rooms and, dreaming, she ran through the dark corridors of her memory, struggling to find a way into the light.

Mercy woke with a start. Someone was knocking at the door, very quietly. She heard a whisper.

"Mercy! Mercy! Can you hear me?"

She jumped out of bed and pressed her ear to the keyhole. "Is that you, Charity? Have you got the key? Can you let me out?"

Mercy heard a scrabbling under the door. Charity was trying to stuff something through the gap.

"There," Charity said. "You've got it. That'll help you get out. I've got to go now. They'll be wondering where I am."

A lump of paper had been thrust under the door. Mercy picked it up. Outside she heard Charity running away down the corridor. The paper had torn, caught on the door, and when Mercy unfolded it, a dull metal key fell from her excited, clumsy fingers to the floor. Mercy scrabbled to pick it up again. Well done, Charity! How had she done it? Had Aurelia a spare that Charity had managed to pocket?

But the key didn't fit the door. She tried it again, wriggling the key in the lock. It was hopeless. The key was far too small. Desolate, she sank back upon the bed, her hands in her lap. Charity had brought the wrong one.

The moon rose in the tiny window, dusting the room with grey light. Mercy rubbed her face. Think, she thought. Think.

The seconds ticked by – then something clicked in Mercy's mind. Intent, she reached for the key's torn paper wrapping, still lying on the floor. She flattened the page, smoothing out the creases.

Drawn on the paper, in quick, black lines, was a map. Mercy's pulse quickened. She strained her eyes, trying to make out the meaning. Clearly Charity had scribbled out the plan in a hurry. It was hard to understand. Mercy turned it one way, and another.

The word "Mercy" was scribbled in one box – obviously the room in which she was trapped. The box's connection with the other rooms was the problem. The map indicated her room had another exit, but Mercy couldn't fathom where it was. Apparently it climbed away from the wall opposite the door. Mercy studied the wall. She stood up and patted it. She stared, biting her lip.

Then the solution dawned, rather horribly. The answer was obvious. Of course the room had another exit – it just hadn't occurred to her to think of it as such. Taking a deep breath, Mercy bent over and stared into the fireplace.

A tiny fireplace it was, too. It hadn't the generous proportions of the hearth in the dining room, or the pretty tiles decorating the fireplace in the nursery parlour. It was plain and mean – suitable only for a servants' room. Would it accommodate a skinny girl?

Mercy looked at the map again. Charity had indicated steps. Mercy stuck her head into the fireplace, and stared up.

At first it made her dizzy. The tunnel ran away. Far up, a disc of dark blue resolved itself into a tiny portion of the night sky. Of course, she was near the top of the house. The roof was not so far away. She withdrew her head and lifted the lamp, to peer at the chimney wall just above the fireplace. The drawing was correct. Steps – of a sort. Bricks stood out, at intervals, providing precarious footholds.

How very narrow it was, black with caked soot, and doubtless inhabited by spiders and beetles. Mercy shuddered. The brick steps were built for the sweeps. Dimly, she remembered them. A man and three little boys coming to the house, exotic creatures in dirty rags. Like monkeys they had shinned up the chimneys, and it had seemed strange and exciting to the girls, as though the sweeps had a trick to perform. Now, considering the climb, Mercy was appalled.

There was nothing for it. If those poor children could do it, so could she. Mercy studied the map again. She took off her dress and bound up her hair, using a piece torn from the old curtains. She tucked the map and the key into her stockings, took a deep breath, and wriggled through the narrow fireplace, and up, into the chimney.

It was lucky she was thin. Even so, squeezing her body through the narrow opening, she scraped her knees and elbows. The fireplace crunched her up, like a black mouth. She dislodged choking clouds of soft, suffocating soot. She thought again of the poor little sweeps.

Once she had scrabbled through the fireplace, the chimney

space opened up a little. The vent joined up with the main chimney, which ran from the ground floor right up to the roof. Mercy found the narrow brick footholds, and began to climb.

It was the hardest and most frightening thing she had ever done. Below her, the chimney plummeted down to the ground, a dizzying distance. Up above, the stars pricked the small circle of night sky. It was bitterly cold, and Mercy's hands were stiff and aching. The soot and dust span from the walls into her eyes and nose and mouth. It was hard to see where she was going.

Step by careful step she climbed, gripping tight with her fingers, hauling herself up, and up. Charity's haphazard map had suggested she rise one floor to what Mercy presumed must be the long attics, coming out through another opening in the chimney.

The climb could only have amounted to a dozen feet. It lasted an eternity for Mercy. Finally, as she stretched her hand to the next brick step, she found instead a small wooden door, just above her head. A door? She pushed it. The door didn't move. She climbed a little higher, so the door was in front of her face. She tried again, banging at each corner, but the door wouldn't budge. She felt all over the surface for a latch or lock. The surface was smooth. Obviously, it could only be opened from the other side.

Mercy was devastated. She couldn't believe it. Why hadn't Charity opened the door? What would she do now, suspended in the chimney high above the ground? She couldn't face the thought of climbing down again, sliding back through the tiny fireplace into her prison. Tears welled.

"Charity!" she called out. "Charity! Help me!"

Silence. She was trapped. What to do now? Should she crawl down again, past her room and beyond, to a lower floor? Already her arms and legs were shaking. Mercy took a deep breath. She climbed a little higher, and pressed her back against the chimney wall opposite the doorway. Her legs were straight in front of her, pressed on the opposite wall, feet either side of the tiny door. Then she drew back one leg – and kicked the door with all her strength.

The door held. Mercy kicked again. Two, three, four. The bang echoed through the confined space, but Mercy didn't relent. She kicked with all her might and frustration.

Five, six! The door flew open, with a clatter, and a cloud of dust. Mercy took a deep breath. She was hot now – and triumphant. She climbed through the space, and collapsed on the bare attic floor.

Slowly she got her breath back. She sat up, wiped her face. Perspiration mingled with the soot, making her eyes sting. She was filthy. Pain from tiny nicks and bruises nipped her legs and arms.

Mercy had no time to feel sorry for herself. She pushed the little door to, but didn't close the latch – just in case. Doubtless, the door, like the brick footholds, had been built to enable the unfortunate child sweeps to clean the chimneys.

She looked about her. Even with her night vision it was hard to see much. The attic had no windows, so she didn't have the benefit of a useful dusting of moonlight. It was a big place, of course, running along the top of the great house. Here and there, lumps of darkness, unwanted furniture and storage crates. A bitter draught blew through the tiles, and Mercy shivered, dressed only in her underclothes.

She started to look for a way out. She used her eyes, and her hands. She felt her way with her feet. Until she had visited that sunny, day-lit Century she had not realised how much she had come to rely on these other senses, to help her negotiate the house. She'd become like someone partially blind – learning the shape of the house, relying on the light of her memory. She could see so well in the dark – like a night creature, an owl or a fox – but a century of wandering had sharpened other senses. What she couldn't see, memory painted in place. Except that she had never been in the attic before. She had no memories to help her out.

She stepped through giant rafters into a second attic room. Here the piles of junk were more crowded. She had to tread carefully. Something scurried, claws rattling on the floorboards. Too big for a mouse? She hugged her arms, and proceeded.

In the jumbled pieces of darkness a flat, draped shape loomed in her path. Could she push it aside? A mothy sheet caught in her fingers when she tried. The object beneath was a sliding stack, hard to move. Three, four things together. No, there were half a dozen, leaning against a wooden crate.

Paintings – they had to be paintings. She read the elaborate frames with her fingers, stroked the smooth, oiled canvas. Could it be the pictures of Thecla and Claudius, the paintings her father couldn't bear to see any more? Of course he would stow them in the attic. It was the obvious place. She touched the canvas with her fingertips. Perhaps she touched her mother's face. A treasure indeed – if this was in fact what she suspected. Her spirits rose. Perhaps her quest wasn't hopeless after all. On top of the pile was a smaller bundle, wrapped in cloth and tied with string. This Mercy picked up and took with her. Another picture, she hoped. A chance to show Charity the faces of her long lost relatives. Her spirits rose. She had come so far. She had overcome what had seemed insurmountable obstacles, relying on her own reserves of strength and courage. And assisted by Charity's ingenuity of course. She had mastered the terrifying chimney! She smiled to herself in the darkness, despite the grit in her eyes and mouth, still clutching the bundle. It was time to go.

She squeezed past the pile of paintings and up a short steep flight of wooden steps to a third room. At the far end she found a little door. She took out Charity's key from her stocking and slipped it into the keyhole. The mechanism grated but the lock turned. Mercy made sure she locked the door again behind her, and kept the key safe. She hurried down a long, narrow stairway to the hallway. Now she had to find Charity.

Charity wasn't in her room. Mercy crept inside and waited. She was black with soot and as cold as ice. She crouched in a corner, huddled up. She had left faint footprints on the carpets. How long till Galatea discovered her captive had fled? She fiddled with the knots binding the bundle from the attic. The string, perished with age, fell apart beneath her fingers. Mercy unfolded the fabric and stared at a delicately fashioned portrait, a white face in the tiny golden frame. She needed to hurry into the Century's past before Trajan or the servants found her again. Perhaps they had discovered Charity was helping her, and locked her up too. She willed Charity to hurry and return.

The door swung open.

"Charity!" Mercy jumped to her feet. Charity was startled. She stared.

"Mercy?" she said. "Look at the state of you. You poor thing. You're filthy. What've you done with your hair?"

"Don't worry. I tied it up, for the climb. See? How did you know about the chimney and the attics?"

"It wasn't easy," Charity said. "I searched in the library for the plans of the house, and the hatchway was marked on, though I worried you wouldn't be able to find it. I stole the attic key from the little cupboard in Aurelia's parlour."

"We haven't much time," Mercy said. "Help me. Give me the book."

Charity still stared. "It just doesn't look like you," she said wonderingly.

Mercy sighed. "Have you some water, so I can wash? And I'll need to borrow some clothes. Then I can escape."

Charity nodded slowly. "You're so different," she said.

"Not just the way you look. You don't even sound like my sister any more."

Mercy took a deep breath. "I know," she said. "I don't feel the same either. Everything is changing. It can't just stay as it was any more. You believe that too, don't you?"

Charity hesitated, then she nodded.

She had a jug of water and a bowl upon the little marble-topped washstand at the end of her room. She poured water into the bowl, while Mercy peeled off her soiled underclothes and stowed them in the bottom of Charity's wardrobe.

She washed as best she could, but the water was cold and there was little of it, and the dust and soot were deeply ingrained. Despite the binding, her hair was full of dust. Charity rummaged for a dress, but her clothes too were elderly and decayed, besides being too small. Mercy took one out, though one sleeve came detached when she pulled it on.

"The book," she said, fastening the buttons that would meet. "Give me the book."

Charity recovered the red book, which she had wrapped in a shawl and stowed beneath her wardrobe.

"Listen carefully," Mercy said. "Father wrote a magic book about Century that keeps us stuck in one long, cold, night. He thinks it will keep us safe, but I don't want to carry on like this, the same day over and over, and I am going to rewrite the story in the red book, to break the spell. His book had pictures in and I think the new book should too. I need you to help me, because you can draw so beautifully. Can you draw the

125

house in the snow with a horseman galloping away? We need a picture of Claudius and Marietta too, and our parents. And pictures of ourselves."

Charity still stared at her elder sister, as though she were struggling to understand what Mercy had told her. Then she shook her head.

"I've never seen Claudius or Marietta – not that I can remember. And I can't remember Mother, either. There aren't any portraits."

"I think they're in the attic," Mercy said. "Father said he locked them away and there is so much up there. I found a stack of pictures when I came through from the chimney. It's the obvious place, isn't it? And look." She picked up the miniature picture, cradling it in her palm. "See? It's Marietta. It belonged to Claudius. It's engraved on the back."

Charity drew a breath. The picture seemed to glow. Marietta, her head turned, regarded them from the tiny portrait. Her youth and beauty glittered, the little picture a window upon another, brighter world.

"She's lovely," Charity breathed. "Like a fairy. Is she real?"

"Yes," Mercy said. "She was real. Claudius loved her. Keep it. Hide it from Father and Galatea. And take a lantern to the attic to find the others. Here's the key. Draw them for me, and I'll come back to collect them. Draw the best pictures you can, and be quick. Make them happy pictures, Charity."

Charity reached out her hands and gripped her sister's arms. "I'm scared, Mercy," she said.

"I am too." Mercy put her arms around Charity and they held each other tight.

"Good luck," Charity said. "I hope you're right."

"We can't live like this," Mercy said. "Just wait. Just wait until you see the day. Then you'll know."

They embraced again, unwilling to let go. Then Mercy pulled away.

"I heard someone," she whispered. "Footsteps. Someone's coming."

"Hide," Charity said. "Quick—"

The handle turned and the door burst open.

"Charity!" Galatea stood in the doorway. She was momentarily at a loss, faced with the two girls – one of them smudged with soot, wearing Charity's dress.

Mercy didn't wait for the governess to gather her wits. She charged at the door, gripping the red book. Mercy was shorter and lighter than Galatea but she had the advantage of speed and surprise. She pushed her out of the way. Galatea let out a high pitched screech, angry and unsettled at once. Mercy didn't stop. She hurtled along the corridor and into the darkness before Galatea could find her balance. Behind her, the governess shouted out, calling for help. Mercy ran past the tall windows, to the unicorn tapestry. Her fingers fumbled against the panelling behind.

"Let me through, please," she prayed. How had she done it before? A matter of will, Claudius had said. Mercy imagined herself in the other place, the library in the sunshine. Galatea was running after her, still shouting. Closer she came. Mercy pulled the tapestry aside and pushed the length of her body against the wood. For a moment the hidden doorway resisted her. She wished for the door to be open. Galatea stretched out a hand to seize. Mercy could smell her peppermint breath – when the panelling suddenly yielded.

Down she went, the in-between time. The space separating one day from the next. One chapter from another.

Far away, Galatea shouted out and stamped her foot.

And Mercy tumbled. Where was this space, she wondered. Head first or feet first – she couldn't really tell. Where was *any* space, come to think of it? You only know where one place is in relation to somewhere else.

She landed in the library. She had her hands pressed over her eyes to shield them from the sunlight. The book was tucked under her arm. This version – her own – could be carried from one sphere to another. Perhaps because it was largely blank. Nothing was fixed. Not yet.

She stood still for a minute or two, gradually releasing her fingers as her eyes grew accustomed to the brightness. She was still out of breath from the chase. Her heartbeat raced. She headed for the shelves of travelogues and maps, to find *The Precise Geography of the Lermantas Archipelago*. Tucked inside the front cover was an ink-stained plan of the house, a fragile, cumbersome document that tore as she unfolded it. A blue cross was marked on the corridor by the tapestry along from her bedroom. A red cross was marked in the library where she had emerged. A second blue cross was drawn on the plan of the first floor – a landing by a window, overlooking the orchard.

She folded the plan and stuffed the book back on the shelf. Time to go. Would Galatea be able to follow her now? Or Trajan, the author of the story of Century?

VII

Mercy hurried through the house. Like a door, the summer day opened before her. Soon the birthday party would begin, while Claudius and Marietta romanced on the island in the middle of the lake. A perfect day. Mercy didn't have time to savour it. She had to pass through to the third of the five days.

She found the landing overlooking the orchard. Outside, a gardener cut back the grass with a long scythe. Mercy climbed onto the window sill and pressed her body against the glass. She emptied her mind and willed the door to let her through. The sun went out.

Hanging in space, she collected her thoughts. Was it just her imagination, or did the gaps grow bigger? The absence of light and place didn't alarm. Instead, the dark space was a comfort, like sleep. Like death, perhaps.

Maybe the gaps widened because she had disrupted Trajan's careful construction. Was that what he meant when he said her movement was unravelling his spell? The chapters were coming part. That would make sense. What about Trajan? Did he tumble in this starless, breathless void? She imagined him, like a ghost, haunting the days of the past, unable to alter what had happened, watching the events rehearse themselves time and again. It was a melancholy image, and perhaps a pitiful one. Trajan, despite his powers, did not have the strength to rise to the challenges of a new life and Mercy's compassion was tempered by impatience – a desire for him to break away from the pain of the past.

She pondered – and hit the floor, ungainly and winded, a heap of bruises. A gloomy room, the faint perfume of a fire. Mercy had landed in front of a hearth, sprawled on a rug. She felt the silky pile beneath her fingers. A chandelier glimmered overhead. She recognised the room as the parlour leading into the hothouses, with its tropical butterflies, and the fish. Mercy shivered. The air was chilly. Not summer any more. She climbed to her feet, picking up the red book from the rug. A gilt-framed mirror darkly reflected her soot-smudged face, the tattered binding about her hair. She wiped her nose on the back of her hand.

"Hurry," she urged the reflection. "We mustn't waste time." But she waited a moment or two longer, staring at the face in the mirror – a face that didn't look familiar any more.

She opened the door beyond the curtains into the hothouse. The long, glass room was crowded with plants and flowers, drowned in a grey twilight. The pale ribs of wood held pieces of the cloudy sky between them. The air was moist and heated. Trajan fed the stoves for his beloved plants, while the servants shivered in their attic rooms. She closed the door again. No one was there. Clearly, the day's story was unfolding elsewhere. A delivery for Claudius, said the little diagram he had drawn, for this chilly autumn day. Mercy would have to find it.

A female servant walked along the corridor, carrying a tray with a silver coffee pot, so Mercy followed. The tall windows revealed a wild morning, very early, the sun low on the horizon and occluded by a rack of cloud. Giant horse chestnut trees grew each side of the long driveway to the house, and they billowed in the wind. Rust- and copper-coloured leaves were torn away. The windows rattled.

Mercy hurried on. The woman, in her dark dress and apron, knocked on a door and went inside. Mercy hovered behind, listening to the voices. Two men. They were quarrelling. She suspected the quieter of the two was her father. The servant put down her tray and hurried out again, away from the angry voices. Mercy crept inside. Probably the quarrellers wouldn't see her, a ghost in the house, but she was careful. Yes – it was Trajan. How different – before the years had fallen on him. His hair was entirely black, like her own. His skin was smooth, his body lean. His eyes shone as he gesticulated to the other man.

"It cannot happen," Trajan said. "You, of all of us, must see why. It's madness! You must put this matter aside, for your own sake – for the family's. For her sake too."

Mercy edged around the other side of the room, where the other man stood behind his desk. It was Claudius. And Claudius, oddly, looked older. A young man, not a youth. His hair was long, tied back with a black ribbon. He wore a stiff, brown apron over his white shirt. The room was some kind of office and laboratory, a long, narrow space with tables covered with books, jars, chemical equipment – and stuffed animals.

"I can overcome the obstacles," Claudius argued. He looked pale and feverish. "When we're married, I'll take Marietta away from Century, from all the suspicious eyes, from her family, to a place where no one knows us – as you've done, bringing your family to England."

"The obstacles can't be overcome." Trajan said. "What life would it be for Marietta, if she could no longer see her family? And how could she bear to grow old and die while you remain as you are? It cannot happen."

"Wait," Claudius urged. "Wait to see what I've planned. Be patient! I'm not as stupid as you think – nor am I so overcome with my emotions that I haven't thought out a solution to the problem. I will satisfy you, Trajan. Give me two months. If my scheme hasn't borne fruit by then, I will do as you say. I will head back to Rome and leave Marietta with her family."

Trajan didn't look satisfied. His hands trembled. He balled his fist, loosened it again. He looked oddly helpless.

"Claudius," he said, more gently now, making an appeal. "Do you think I don't understand what it is to love someone? When I fell in love with Thecla I knew she would be the bright star of my life, that nothing would have any meaning without her." He stretched out his arm, to pat his brother upon the shoulder, to comfort, but Claudius pulled away.

"If you understand, why won't you help me?" he said.

"Because I am thinking of Marietta! What plan can you have that can possibly overcome this difficulty? Nothing can be done!" Trajan said. He looked at Claudius, angry and afraid at once. Mercy sensed his frustration – his inability to force the younger man to obey him. Was he, despite his extraordinary sorcerous powers, the weaker of the two?

"Nothing can be done," he said again, voice failing. "Think on it. Think of *her*."

Then he left the room. He closed the door behind him with a bang. Mercy shivered, standing by the wall.

Claudius sighed. He stretched, rose to his feet and took a few steps around the room, restless, shaking off the argument. Books were heaped haphazardly on shelves. Piles of notes lay jumbled on the table. Glass beakers, tubes and retorts clustered on a bench at the back of the room, stained with curious residues and crusts of coloured crystals. And the animals. Some stood posed in glass cases, others on wooden stands. A fox, a badger, a tiny deer. A tawny owl, a pheasant. A long trout, like a sword. Their sad glass eyes stared at Mercy, as if the dead creatures could see her, when the living could not. She reached out a hand to touch the fox's coat, burning red like the horse chestnut leaves outside. She stroked its smooth, hard back. On the other side of the room, Claudius was staring out of the window, lost in thought. Abruptly he turned around and rifled through the papers on his desk. He began to write notes.

Stirred by Mercy's caress, a cloud of dust had lifted from the fox. The motes spun. Mercy's nose tickled. She held her breath – but the sensation increased. She was going to sneeze.

The sudden noise broke the silence in the room. Mercy put her hands to her face and stared at Claudius in alarm. He was still writing at his desk. He gave no indication that he had heard. The moments passed. Slowly, she relaxed and walked right up to his desk. She stared at the papers. He was writing a letter – addressed to Marietta. Chemical formulae, strings of Greek letters and drawings of bones and joints covered other pages strewn on the desk. Claudius continued to write.

"Can you see me now, Claudius?" Mercy whispered.

Claudius lifted his head and nodded. "Yes," he said. "You've come from the future to set me free." Then he returned to his writing, ignoring her. Perhaps it was an effort for him, to notice her. He was caught up in the pattern of the story. He had told her it took all his strength to cross from one day to another, to seek her out. Mercy turned away, walked across the room, and opened the door.

She wandered round the house. Everything was quiet. She found the sisters in the kitchen eating porridge and honey, and afterwards, followed them into the garden, down to the grand arboretum, where they ran around in the wind.

She remembered her father planting the trees. The scene

rose up. The avid collection of foreign species, the men embedding the young trees in the cold English earth, Trajan barking nervous instructions. Enthused, like a boy, he had taught her the names of the trees. Lebanon cedars, black walnuts from the New World. Later, from Australia, they planted tea trees and bottlebrush, and in the heart where concentric paths met, a grove of magnolia trees, where the white flowers opened like waxy cups in the spring. Now the trees were still immature. At home, she remembered, in her own Century, the arboretum was vast, the trees dank and overgrown.

The girls went in again. Mercy sat on the stone stairway at the front of the house. What was going to happen? She opened her red book and read through the first pages of her account. So many dangling threads. Why did Trajan and Thecla oppose the marriage with Marietta? Because the family was different. Her experience of human life was, she understood too well, very limited. She had read a great many books. She had lived, so it seemed, more than a hundred years. Sleeping Beauty had slept a hundred years, though the Bible suggested a man might live just three score years and ten. Which stories should she trust? Trajan had warned Claudius that Marietta would grow old and die, while he remained unchanged.

What would it be like to live for hundreds of years? She tested the idea in her mind. She had never thought about dying. And though she might already have lived for a century, because of Trajan's enchantment it had only seemed like a day. If the spell were broken and she began to live again, in an ever-changing world, then whole centuries tunnelled away in front of her. Long years, with only her immortal family as constant companions, while other, ordinary people would flit in and out of her life, as they grew up, aged and died. She had once loved Chloe. Presumably, in the outside world, Chloe had grown up. Perhaps she had married and become an old lady and then passed away. So now she must be lying in a grave. Mercy felt an unbearable pang of loneliness, to think of it. She had already lost so much.

She began to understand how such a lifespan would set them apart, if other people failed and died in a handful of decades. How lonely it could be. Mercy rubbed her arms. The too-small dress chafed. Her hands were cold and white. She had so little sense of time. She had repeated the same actions over and over for a hundred years. Not much of a life, for all its length.

How was Thecla's disappearance embroidered into the story of the lovers? How did Claudius think he could overcome his fate, and marry Marietta? And why did he fail? This wild, stormy day in autumn held a vital chapter in the tale. What was it?

Far away, along the main drive through the tunnel of trees, a dark shape moved beside the gatehouse. Mercy narrowed her eyes, straining to see. A wagon, travelling fast. It took some minutes for the wagon to be close enough to see the carter, who was sat up at the front in a big brown coat. The horse was a heavy bay, with a white stripe on its face and four feathery white socks. The wagon was covered. Behind her, the front door opened. Mercy turned to see Claudius hurrying out, down the stairs, to greet the new arrival. His boots clacked on the stone. He was still dressed in the brown apron. Mercy stood up and followed him.

Just before the house the carter suddenly reined in the horse. The large, yellowish hooves kicked up the gravel. The creature's neck was slick with sweat, its nostrils flared. The carter jerked the reins again and the horse tossed its head.

"Go to the side of the house, to the stable yard," Claudius ordered. "One of the men will help you unload. Did you bring everything?"

The carter nodded, a stout, red-faced man in middle age. The horse fretted, clamping its teeth on the bit. The whip cracked and the wagon turned. Claudius headed into the house, Mercy on his heels. He strode through the hallway, called for one of the footmen, and cut through a side door into the stable yard, where the carriers brought supplies for the kitchen. The wagon was pulling up on the cobbled ground.

"Over here!" Claudius half-ran to the wagon, the footman hurrying to keep up. The carter threw back the heavy cover from his load, a half dozen wooden crates. He jumped down from his high seat and lowered the back of the wagon. Claudius and the footman took the crates, one by one, to the doorway.

"Take them to the second floor, and leave them outside my room," Claudius said. "Don't let them fall."

The footman, in royal blue jacket and white wig, nodded nervously. A strong-looking young man, he struggled under the weight of the first crate. Claudius turned to the carter. He took gold coins from his pocket.

"As we agreed," he said.

"And for my trouble?" The carter was rough-looking. His voice was gruff. He stepped closer to Claudius. The horse shifted its hooves behind them. Claudius sneered. Although the shorter of the two, he drew himself up straight and seemed to loom over the carter. The man's bluff face reddened, and he stepped back. Claudius dug into his pocket again, drew out more gold. The coins passed from his long, white hand into the beefy red fist of the carter.

"Thank you sir," the carter said, touching the front of his hat. He struggled to regain his composure but his smile was disrespectful. He backed away from Claudius and climbed up to the front of the wagon.

"If you need me again, sir, you know where to find me." He picked up the whip and cracked it over the horse's head. The wagon rumbled over the cobbles, and out of the yard.

Claudius picked up the second box and carried it inside. Mercy followed him up a narrow servants' stairway to the second floor. She wasn't familiar with this part of the house. So much had been locked up by the time her winter's day began. They passed accommodation for the footmen and the coachman. The floorboards in the narrow passageway were bare. She glimpsed a plain little room with two beds side by side. The servant had just deposited the first crate outside a door at the end of the passage. He waited for Claudius.

"I'll take it inside," Claudius said. "Fetch the next box."

Visibly perspiring, the young man nodded and hurried off. Claudius unfastened a pocket in his breeches and drew out an elaborate key. He unlocked the door, and moved the crates inside. Mercy slipped past him, and surveyed a second, secret laboratory.

It was a long, unadorned room with a closed door at the far end. Two mean windows provided a poor amount of light. Ranks of candles were posted at each end of an expansive table, on a wrought-iron candelabra, as well as stuck on any convenient surface – such as the glass case in which an iron-coloured pike was preserved, and a box of butterflies pinned in careful rows. Mercy moved to the table. Claudius had arrayed his tools on a series of wooden trays. At the other end, a fat, frayed leather-bound book rested on a pile of notes. Here and there drawings were pinned on the bare walls – anatomical studies of animals. The articulation of joints. The web of muscle in a human thigh. Mercy was intrigued and revolted.

Claudius was still busy with the crates, so Mercy placed her red book on the floor beneath the table and flicked open the cover of Claudius's book. She glanced at the first page, and her heart sank. Claudius, dedicated scientist, had written his notes in Latin. So much the harder for her! She took a deep breath, composed her thoughts, and endeavoured to find the right frame of mind to tackle his untidy writing and the difficult language.

The first pages dated from 1660. Diagrams of plants, curious patterns of symbols. To begin with, Claudius had taken up alchemy to understand the nature of life – the animating force that set a blade of flowering grass apart from a piece of straw. Or a plank of wood from a vital tree. Jotted notes littered the pages. Some simply contained lists of letters. She turned the pages. At the turn of the century, the time she thought her parents had moved to England, Claudius had apparently travelled to the Middle East. His notes referred to Morocco, Egypt and Persia. He had written from cities – Algiers, Cairo, Luxor. Notes in Arabic interspersed the Latin – as well as hieroglyphics copied from the walls of Egyptian tombs and sketches of the resurrected god Osiris. Claudius had learned the art of mummification, evidenced by detailed drawings and notes covering dozens of pages. Two years later, he travelled to Prague to research the tale of Rabbi Low Ben Bazalel, who made a golem in 1590 – a man made of clay and brought to life when the rabbi put a slip of paper under its tongue bearing the sacred word Shem.

The notes died away during the middle years of the 18th century. Perhaps Claudius had tired of his studies. Perhaps he had whiled away a decade or two in poetry, or hunting, or indolence. It was strange a man gifted with such longevity should have spent so much time wrestling with the problem of death and rebirth. Then again, the studies were also a quest for an origin. Claudius was trying to understand how he – and consequently the Verga family as a whole – had cheated the destiny meted out to every other plant, creature and human being on the face of the earth. Who were they? Why did the family possess such a treasury of special talents?

Mercy ploughed on. The notes started again in earnest at the tail end of 1788, just one year earlier. Before she could read more, Claudius banged the door shut and drew across two thick black bolts. The six crates stood around him, nailed shut. The stamps of foreign ports were daubed on the raw wood. Claudius surveyed them, one by one; the patient boxes waiting for his attention. He picked up an iron stake from the table and jammed it beneath the lid of the first crate, which came from Venice. The wood split, the nails screeched, as he wrenched off the top. Inside, packed carefully in straw, lay a smooth glass egg. He threw handfuls of straw on the floor, and lifted the vessel with reverence. One long pipe provided the only ingress into the fine glass bubble. Claudius held the vessel to the light, admiring. He used a wooden rule to measure it.

"Beautiful," he said aloud. "So beautiful. They've excelled themselves. It's perfect – just as I asked." He replaced the vessel gently in the nest of straw and set to work on the other boxes. A second, bearing the Venetian stamp, disgorged other, smaller pieces of glassware and two balls of coloured glass, in a padded velvet box. Other crates contained books of dense text, folders of parchment, bolts of cloth, tubes of fabric filled with coloured crystals and powders, bottles of various liquids, and strangest of all, the most remarkable dress that Mercy had ever seen.

Claudius lifted the dress from the last crate. Mercy couldn't

143

identify the stamp. The letters might have been Russian. The dress unfolded without a sound. Mercy took a breath. She recalled folk tales where fairies and devoted mothers embroidered gowns made of moonlight and spider silk, star flowers, dew drops. The dress was white, grey and silver – though bald names for colour did not aptly describe the arcane mesh of pearl, snowdrop, sea mist, frost. A winter's dress. A wedding dress. Claudius embraced the gown, as though his bride-to-be were already inside it. He ran his fingers over the embroidered surface, the web of tiny gems. He pressed his face into the cold silk drop of the skirts. How much he loved Marietta. Mercy could see it now, written in the tenderness he lavished on the dress he had bought to adorn her, in the rapture on his face.

He took the dress to the end of the long room and unlocked the door. Mercy caught a last glimpse of the dress as he placed it in an oak chest. He stroked it once more, and returned to the laboratory, locking the door again behind him. He stood by the table, gazing at the long line of implements, lost in thought. The wind pressed at the window. A few fat raindrops splattered against the glass. A shower ripened into a downpour, within minutes. The gloomy room darkened, and Claudius began to light the forest of candles. Fresh wax trickled from the flame, fingered a path over the congealed rivulets of earlier burnings, to set in new and grotesque shapes at the base of the candle, on the table and cabinets, and the floor.

Claudius stood in his halo of flame and flicked through the notes in his leather-covered book. He began to work.

Mercy crouched against the wall to watch. A current of thought or passion had galvanised Claudius now. He began the long and painstaking task of assembling his equipment, using the new components from the crates as well as older pieces he already possessed. He snatched down diagrams from the walls and referred again to his old notes. He pored at length over pages in the new books. He didn't once look away from the job in hand. He was intent – a man possessed. He became the process, reading and assimilating, building and taking apart, writing and reassessing.

The candles burned down, and were replaced. The rain passed over, and briefly the autumn sun burst through the cloud, so the drops on the window glittered.

Claudius burned a yellow powder in a stone dish. The smoke was acrid at first, then sweet, like jasmine. He stirred the resultant ash into a clear liquid, sprinkled on tiny crystals, a dried-blood red. He cleared the table and used the potion as an ink to draw symbols on its pitted surface. A circle, cardinal points, intervals marked with glyphs. He rearranged the network of glass tubes, leading into the Venetian egg, hatched from the first crate. At last he stood back. Everything, apparently, was ready.

What now? Mercy stirred, back stiff, her legs cramped. She stretched out her limbs and clambered to her feet. What now? Mercy waited in the shadows, mesmerised.

Claudius ran his eyes over the assembly once more, and took a deep breath, in and out. His face was very pale, hectic dabs of colour high on his cheeks. His lips were almost white. He pushed his hair from his face. Reaching some inner decision, he turned from the table and disappeared again into the next room. He returned with a closed basket, inside of which a creature shifted and made a curious sobbing sound.

Claudius put the basket on the table and spoke some reassuring words to the animal inside. A white-and-tabby cat pressed its face plaintively against the wickerwork and miaowed. Mercy pressed her fingernails into her palm in sudden apprehension – what was he going to do? The cat continued to miaow, circling in the confines of the basket, as the man made a final trip into the other room, returning with a stuffed animal in his hands. He placed it at the end of the table. Mercy moved closer, to take a look.

No, it wasn't yet another work of taxidermy – though the science was something akin to it. Claudius had constructed a cat replica. A complex work of engineering. The replica was half-covered in black fabric; face, body and two legs. The other half remained unskinned, exposing the cunning workings of the construct – crafted from wood and ivory, copper wires, pockets stuffed (perhaps with sawdust) providing bulk, and rheumy amber eyes, like the stuffed animals in cases.

Mercy could hardly breathe. Her heart pattered, seemingly in her throat.

Claudius placed the cat in the basket in the centre of the circle inscribed on the surface of the table. He opened one of the new books, and drew out a sheet of parchment, brown with age and water-stains. He stepped back, stood up straight, and began to read aloud.

Mercy could neither understand the words nor calculate the origin of the language. The words, however, seemed to screw themselves through her hair and into her brain. Sacred words. Words of power, like Shem, written on a slip of paper under the golem's tongue. Didn't God summon the universe from the void with the power of his words?

Claudius continued to read. The outside world disappeared, space contracted to the four walls, the table, the cat yowling in the basket. The candles blazed as one, and extinguished, filling the room with smoke. Instead, a cold blue light shone from the inked-out circle, illuminating the room. The tools on the table rattled. A book flew in the air, pages turning and turning. Mercy felt the bones of her skull grind together. Still Claudius proceeded.

The cat screeched one last time, and was still. The blue light flared, and a smaller cobalt ball of intense brightness emerged from the back of the cat's throat, over its tongue, to be caught in a glass funnel which directed the dazzling, fluid light along the glass tube. Slowly the piece of light crept along the tube, seemingly reluctant to move. Inch by steady inch, the blue light progressed, until it dropped, like a stone, into the belly of the Venetian egg.

Upon the walls the butterflies pinned in cases fluttered their wings. The pike in the glass case snapped its jaws, curved its long body from side to side. The floorboards groaned, nails popping.

Claudius was losing strength now. The magic had damaged him. Blood trickled from his left nostril, over his lip. A window pane cracked, and another. The cobalt light swam about in the glass vessel, shaping itself into the tiny likeness of a cat.

The stream of words came to an end. In an instant Claudius pulled away the glass pipe and jammed a wooden stopper in the vent to contain the cat spirit. His face was jubilant. He wiped the blood from his nose, purple bruises now rising around his eyes and mouth. Did he feel any pain? He gave no sign of it, shoving the basket and the drained cat body to the floor without a thought. The blue radiance was fading, and he relit a dozen candles. The butterflies still twitched. The pike flapped feebly, baring rows of needle teeth.

Claudius moved the artificial cat into the circle. He adjusted the apparatus, replacing the glass pipe with another, directed into the throat of the cloth cat. He crouched, to stare at the luminous blue spirit in the vessel; the tiny cat that jumped, and sprawled on its back and batted invisible motes with its front feet.

"The animating spirit," he whispered. "The Egyptians called it the *ka*. The eskimos called it the *Inua*. The immortal soul. Does a cat have a smaller *ka* than a man, I wonder?"

He moved from side to side, peering at the cat soul. He checked the arrangement of pipes and stoppers once more and picked up a second piece of parchment from the old book.

Mercy braced herself, prepared for the words to tear and

rend. She stuck her fingers in her ears. Claudius turned a cunning gate in the new glass pipe and began to speak.

This time the words were gentle, for the remaking. The tight-wound tension in the room relaxed. The butterflies and fish in their cases became still and lost their half life. The words soothed. Outside, a last flash of sunshine seeped through the window, dusting the multifarious objects in the room with gold. The little soul, with a sound like a sigh, was sucked from the vessel along the downward pipe and into the throat of the cloth cat. The last gleam of blue went out. Claudius put the parchment down. The room was perfectly still.

Mercy began to breathe easily again. Claudius dabbed his face with his white sleeve, the blood still dripping from his nose. He looked dreadful, with the bruises blossoming. A skein of hair at his left temple had turned white.

Claudius turned his attentions to the cloth cat. He sealed the hole in its throat with a piece of parchment, and stitched a flap of fabric over.

"Wake up," he said. "Wake up."

The cat still flopped – merely a haphazard collection of wood and cloth and sawdust. Claudius stroked its face. Shook it.

"Wake up," he tried again. He stepped back. Expressions of expectation and anxiety struggled in his face. The cloth cat didn't move. A minute passed, and another. The cloth cat twitched its tail. Mercy could scarcely believe her eyes. Claudius stared. The tail twitched again. The cat seemed to sneeze. Its legs moved in a quick convulsion. It lifted its head, and looked around. Sleepily, it struggled to its feet, off-balance and lopsided. It swayed on its four feet, then jumped from the table to the floor, falling clumsily on its side when it hit the ground. The cloth cat clambered to its feet again, and wandered, like a drunk, around the room. Its movements, however, were uncannily cat-like. Bisected, half cloth-covered, half articulated skeleton and exposed stuffing, it was a horror.

Claudius tipped back his head and laughed. He was a horror too, with his damaged face and sleeve blotted with blood. He danced on the floor, and jabbed his fists in the air. He left the cat to its cautious exploration, and hurried into the adjoining room. Mercy followed.

A long wooden chest bound with iron rested against a wall, under a window. The chest was fastened with a padlock the size of a man's fist. Claudius sank to his knees and applied a key to the lock. With reverence, he lifted the lid. Mercy crossed the room to stand behind him, looking over his shoulder. The lid dropped back against the wall. Claudius folded back a piece of fine white silk – to reveal the most beautiful, remarkable thing she had, or would ever, see.

The plan became apparent at once.

Inside the chest lay a silk doll with long, auburn hair. Marietta, perfected. A flawless, bewitching creation with slim, supple limbs. Her artificial skin possessed a dewy glimmer. Her lips, a rosebud, were slightly parted. Her hands lay crossed across her chest.

How had Claudius created such a being? Her beauty was beyond human. She was an angel. A goddess.

Doubtless, inside the silken skin, flesh of sawdust and horsehair was built upon a skeleton of ivory and wood, like the cloth cat. It was hard to imagine such ordinary goods were contained within the silk purse of the angel doll, with its pearl fingernails and petal eyelids, drawn over eyes of sapphire and glass.

Claudius stared and smiled. He reached out to touch the doll's face, then remembering the filth upon his hands he snatched his fingers back again.

"Soon," he said. "Soon, Marietta, we shall be together for ever."

VIII

The dark October evening was drawing on. A girl with a basket of kindling and coal came into the library and knelt before the hearth, to set the fire. The clock on the mantelpiece chimed the half hour.

Mercy was sitting at her father's desk in the library. A red book, embossed with gold, lay on the table before her. It was Trajan's *Century*, like the one she had seen in the library on the summer day, telling the story that held the enchantment together. And like the other one, it possessed a supernatural glitter. When she turned the pages, a peculiar sensation crackled along her fingers, and over her skin. She thought it was the same, singular book – not a duplicate. Like a magical stitch it ran through Trajan's cage of days, holding them together.

Trajan's first chapters made sense to her now. She skimmed the pages, and read about the arrival of the Vergas in England. In 1700 Trajan and Thecla sent an agent from Italy to buy up the land for their new house and named the estate for the turning of the new century. Later, the house was built, and the couple moved to England. The children were born. Then the story told of the meeting of Claudius and Marietta, the disagreement between the brothers, and the arcane plan concocted by Claudius to grant Marietta eternal life. Further on though, the writing stopped making sense. The lines would not resolve themselves into words. Perhaps the spell protected itself and she would not be able to read the story until she had discovered for herself how the events would unfold.

Mercy took up her own red book and placed it on the table beside the one her father had written. A pen and ink waited by her right hand, but Mercy could not bring herself to write. She had no time to lose. She remembered that when the summer day ended, as she spoke with Claudius on the island, she had been sucked back to her own time without wishing for it – and without the need for a door. Soon the autumn day would end and presumably she would find herself dropped back in the summer day, even at home in midwinter. And if she was returned to her own time, against her wishes, Trajan would surely lock her up so tight she would never get another chance to complete this journey into the past. She had no time to lose. Despite this sense of urgency, Mercy continued to stare at the book.

The nightmare of the day's events held her mind and heart in a tight grip. The yowls of the tabby-and-white cat. Its soft body flopping in the basket when the *ka* was torn out. The sight of the animated cloth and sawdust creation staggering around the room. Claudius, his wild face smudged with blood and bruises, and the dead pike struggling in its case. And the doll too. Yes, the angel doll with its unholy, bewitching beauty. The memory burned.

It was all too much. She didn't know what to think. Couldn't think. The pathways of her mind had jammed up. Her heartbeat echoed in her ears. She was all alone and she had no one to turn to. She felt very small, facing a matter too big and too difficult to deal with.

The clock chimed the quarter hour. Must leave. Must move on to the next day. Still she stared at the book.

Trajan had been right.

Claudius was a monster. Such a man was rightly locked up in the spiral of days past. She would be a fool to set him free – even if in so doing she regained her own life, and that of her sister. Why hadn't she trusted her father? Maybe her own dark imprisonment was a price worth paying to keep Claudius at a distance from the world. He had no conscience. He was capable of anything.

Two days still remained, and Mercy didn't know whether to proceed on her journey through the Verga family's troubled past. Perhaps she should return home, hand over the red book, and hope Trajan could sew up the seams she had torn in his web of days. On the other hand, questions still nagged. She longed to find out the truth about her mother. How was Thecla involved in this? Had she died, as Trajan had told her?

How had Claudius's careful, diabolical plan come to pieces? And could she be certain that the confinement of Claudius was really worth the endless, dead-end lives of Charity, Trajan and herself? Was she misjudging him? He had acted out of love. Such love for Marietta. Mercy remembered his face, when he stroked the dress. Mad for love. Maybe such love was another word for selfishness and obsession. Claudius should have left Marietta, to enjoy an ordinary life. Or, if he had loved her truly, he would have treasured a mortal marriage, and loved Marietta even as she aged and died.

It was no good. No matter how often she turned the facts around, no matter how she considered and weighed up the information in her hand, no easy answer emerged. She couldn't see a way through. Only one course of action remained. She would have to discover the turn of events in the next two days. Maybe then, armed with greater knowledge, she would reach an informed conclusion.

Mercy stood up, took up her red book, and found *The Precise Geography of the Lermantas Archipelago* among the travelogues and books of maps. The plan folded inside the cover indicated the doorway she had come through in the parlour by the hothouse – and the next doorway in a guest bedroom on the first floor, not far from Thecla's rooms. Again, it didn't indicate where she would emerge. Now she was afraid she had left too little time before the end of the day, and that it might all fold up and cast her out. Mercy shoved *The Precise Geography* back on the shelf and ran through the corridors and up the stairs.

Thank goodness the bedroom was easy to find. The room contained a huge bed. Dark wooden panelling lined the walls. The doorway should be to the left – halfway along. Mercy tucked her book under her arm and felt her away along the smooth wood. She inched her way. The night was coming upon them. She had to be quick. She cleared her mind, recalled the sensation of falling – and the door opened. Her hands plunged through the wall, and Mercy stumbled forwards into the gap between the days. Her tatty dress fluttered. The book slipped from her arm. The moment stretched. And stretched. Mercy's thoughts streamed away.

She landed in the corridor, by the stag-and-unicorn tapestry. Everything was dark and cold. Mercy got onto her knees, still hunched over. She picked up the red book, from the floor by her side. So cold. A draught ran along the corridor, prickling her arms. The taste of the winter air was too familiar. She could smell the frost – in a panic. She hadn't been quick enough. Had the day ended, snapped shut, before she reached the next chapter? Surely, she was home again, in her own time.

Mercy climbed to her feet, dismayed. Her heart was heavy. How could this have happened? Hadn't she been quick enough?

Trajan and Galatea would not let her escape again and she would never find out what happened at the end of the story. Mercy felt utterly wretched. Having resolved to carry on, it was unbearable to have the quest snatched away. Slowly she walked along the corridor towards her room. The windows revealed a sky awash with a glittering flood of stars.

She stared out, hearing footsteps in the corridor. Resigned, Mercy waited for Galatea to arrive. The footsteps drew nearer. Mercy turned, to see not one, but two slim figures walking towards her. The taller of the two carried a candle.

"The sun will rise soon." The bearer of the candle was a woman, in a servant's dress and a white cap. "We'll be busy. Fires must be set in every room. There's so much to do."

The women walked straight past Mercy, without seeing her. And Mercy allowed herself a little smile. Those servants were not from her own time. This wasn't 1890 after all. It was a winter from the past. The journey continued. A whole new day lay before her.

The family were still abed. One of the servants knocked on the door of Thecla's bedroom, to light the fire so the room would be warm when she dressed. Mercy peeped in, to see her parents lying together in the carven bed. A sweep of Thecla's golden hair lay across the pillow. Her head was resting on Trajan's chest. How peaceful they looked. Trajan's face was soft and sleepy. Thecla whispered something to him, and he laughed, and kissed her on the top of her head, lifting her hand in his, fingers threaded.

Mercy stared. They were so close, but so far away. She could stand beside them and shout and still they wouldn't hear her. She was all on her own. She pulled herself away and left the room.

Mercy began to search for Claudius, but his laboratory rooms were locked and she could find no evidence he was sleeping in one of the many guest rooms. She also looked in the library, to find *The Precise Geography* and the location of the doorway into the final, central day, and found – oddly – that it lay in her own bedroom, behind the dressing table. She committed the plan to memory.

The clock on the mantelpiece chimed eight times. Outside, the sky paled, the sun about to rise over the bare trees and fields of frost. In the distance, a solitary deer lifted its head from the iced grass and seemed to stare at the window where Mercy stood.

She went downstairs, to the kitchen, which even at this early hour bustled with life and activity. Aurelia and half a dozen assistants were hard at work preparing for a great festivity. In the fireplace a giant spit roast turned. A skinny woman with a sweaty face was preparing a pudding, pouring off-white batter into a bag of muslin. The firelight glinted off bright copper moulds hanging from racks above the long table. A young woman chopping herbs put down her knife to shoo away a ginger cat, which took a dignified leap to the top of the dresser. The air smelled of nutmeg and ginger, wine and bitter chocolate. Two girls, of about ten or twelve, plucked feathers from limp pheasants lying across their laps. A further half-dozen birds lay in a pile on the floor, awaiting their attentions. A short, stout man hacked at a long pig's carcass on a wooden bench at the back of the room. A couple of terriers fretted at his feet, waiting for a scrap. There was scarcely space to move and, despite the cold outside, the kitchen was hot as a furnace.

Mercy hovered at the edge of this hive of industry, eavesdropping. The servants, while under pressure, were excited. A great event was about to unfold. Soon the house would be full of people. The Vergas would host a grand midwinter party. All the local families would attend. While the lady and master of the house prepared themselves, the tribe of servants, the powerhouse of the kingdom of Century, would clean, cook, decorate and adorn, serve the guests, and afterwards clear up all the mess. Some of the treats would reach them however – the servants would also dine well today. They would glimpse the fine dresses of the visitors. A band of musicians was due to attend, and perhaps the servants might hear them play. Yes, for all the work, the party would provide some entertainment and colour in the long, dark winter day.

Mercy retreated to the familiar surroundings of the library, where Trajan's *Century* rested on a desk. She stroked the red cover with her fingertips. The book looked a little jaded this time, the pages yellow at the edges. Maybe she was absorbing its power into her own book, undoing Trajan's spell, page by painstaking page.

She reached for the pen and ink, curled her legs on the chair, opened her own red book and began to write about the events of the previous day. She recounted everything she knew, interspersed with her own thoughts and doubts. By the time she had finished, a bright blue sky filled the window. The frost on the branches began to melt and slide away.

Little Mercy and Charity rushed into the room later in the morning, to eat a meal of bread and cheese, with slices of apricot from the hothouse. The girls chattered and squabbled, anticipating the arrival of friends. Galatea, still stern, came into the room and scolded them for the noise. Charity's hair was curled with cloth, to bring out her ringlets. Mercy listened to their chatter wistfully. Their dresses were so smart and clean. The girls were bright with expectation. How thrilling to go to a party, to welcome guests, to dance and listen to music. Despite her misgivings, Mercy couldn't help but share the girls' excitement.

The guests would be driven to the house in the early afternoon. The party would proceed through the long, solstice night until dawn the next day. Century had never beheld anything like this celebration. No one mentioned Claudius, or Marietta, though little Mercy talked of Chloe at length.

The girls were ushered from the nursery parlour to their rooms to prepare. Mercy tucked the red book beneath her chair, and set off to find her mother.

Thecla was in her bedroom. In the fireplace, flames danced over logs scented with apple. Thecla's maidservant dressed her hair, while Thecla considered her reflection. Mercy sat on the edge of the great bed, catching a glimpse of her own ragamuffin appearance: soot-smudged face, torn dress and mass of tangled hair. The maidservant piled up Thecla's sleek

161

hair, pinned it with pearls, ornaments of holly berries and tiny ivy leaves. Thecla whitened her face with powder, painted her lips red and stuck a tiny velvet heart upon her right cheek. Then she stood in her undergarments and a hooped petticoat, while the maidservant took a vast holly-green dress from the wardrobe. Painstakingly, she lifted the gown over Thecla's head, fastened the host of tiny buttons at the back of the tight bodice top, and fussed over the spill of skirts spreading over the petticoat.

Thecla regarded herself in the mirror, turning to consider the outfit from every angle.

"You are beautiful." Trajan stepped into the room, reaching out to embrace his wife. The maid stepped aside, and left the room.

"Look," he said, proudly, opening a leather box. "Will you wear them tonight?" Upon a cushion of silver velvet lay a handful of fat, red gems. Mercy had seen the jewels in paintings still hanging in the house, fastened around the necks of Vergas from the past, her female ancestors. Now Trajan fixed the necklace about Thecla's powdered neck, where the jewels smouldered.

"How do you feel?" Thecla said, touching the gems with her fingertips. "Do you think we shall be a success?"

"I confess – I do feel nervous," he said. "We've kept so much to ourselves. It is a risk, isn't it, welcoming so many people? Are you sure this was a wise idea?"

"Making a spectacle of ourselves," Thecla mused. "In any

case, we shall have to move again, at some time, back to the old country. When people start to notice how little we change."

"We've plenty of time. The years for the children to grow up," Trajan said, reassuring himself. "Better for them to stay here."

Thecla picked up a silk fan, painted with roses.

"The guests will arrive soon," Trajan said.

"Still no sign, then, of Claudius?"

Trajan shook his head. "Perhaps he's come to his senses. Marietta's father told me they were keeping the girl in her room."

"It was a cruel thing you did," Thecla considered. "To tell her family Claudius wasn't to be trusted. That he had previous . . . commitments."

"A cruel thing. A necessary thing."

Mercy watched as her parents exchanged a significant look.

"We were blessed, to find each other," Thecla said. "Do you remember the day our parents introduced us, when we were children, in the big house in the old country?"

"Without you, I would be so much dust blowing in the wind. You are everything. You, and our daughters."

They stood, face to face, holding hands. Trajan seemed to search his wife's face.

"Will you tire of me, one day, down the long path of centuries?" she said, smiling, knowing the answer.

"Not in a thousand years, nor ten thousand," he said.

Mercy's heart seemed to contract, seeing the love and youth on her father's face and remembering the tense, angry, broken thing he had become.

Some commotion broke out downstairs. Mercy ran past her parents and downstairs, to the hallway. A black carriage had drawn up at the bottom of the stone stairs, beyond the grand front door. Another carriage waited behind it, and a third was visible, progressing along the drive. The guests were arriving.

Bleak midwinter, the tail end of 1789. The house glittered with candles. A hundred guests, dressed in their finery. The men had powdered their hair with nutmeg and gold dust. The women, like exotic flowers, wore dresses of fine silk and embroidered velvet. Swags of shining ivy adorned the house. Bouquets of holly and pom-poms of mistletoe tied with gold ribbon hung from the walls. Spiced with white roses, evergreens stretched along the dining-room table, laden with a monstrous feast.

A roast peacock, tail-feathers in a fan. Platters of stuffed pigeons. Veal in a sauce, roast pheasant, pork chops in spice. Puddings of trout and pike, a mottled block of Stilton. Towering cakes, meringues and iced mille-feuilles.

A chamber orchestra played Mozart in an adjoining room, where people might dance. The guests discussed the terrors of the French Revolution.

Mercy, incongruous in her dirt and rags, wandered unseen among the revellers, a tatty ghost at the party. Little Mercy, dressed in her finest gown stitched with ruby-coloured roses, ran around the house in pursuit of the beloved Chloe, who darted among the guests, laughing. She skipped up the stairs. The girls were playing hide-and-seek. Intrigued, Mercy followed her younger self. Watching the girls play, she remembered again what it felt like to have a friend. Memories stirred, like a dark door opening on a sunny garden. Mercy had loved Chloe with a passion. They talked endlessly. They laughed together, side by side. They spent the long summer evenings exploring the gardens and the arboretum. Chloe was Mercy's other half. Her scintillant, optimistic opposite. If she succeeded, and the house was free again, would she ever have another friend?

Now it was little Mercy's turn to hide. She ran off, while Chloe stood outside the bedroom, counting and laughing. Chloe covered her face with her fingers, but she peeped, and finally set off in search of her friend. Mercy was about to follow, when she heard a rap on the great doors at the front of the house. It was late now, and dark for travelling. She ran to the tall windows. A small carriage, lamps at the front, was drawing away from the house. Who had just arrived?

Downstairs, the party hubbub had died away. The musicians played on, while the women congregated in the hallway, whispering behind their fans, as the doors opened. Mercy pushed her way to the front. Claudius stood outside, Marietta by his side. She wore the white and pearl dress from the Russian crate, like a princess. She had a fine gold ring on her finger.

Mercy gasped – and looked among the gathering for her parents.

A path opened among the assembly as Trajan and Thecla appeared. Just behind them stood Marietta's father, a gaunt, plain man, cheeks scarred by the smallpox. Trajan sought to quell the emotion playing across his face. Outrage, apprehension. He looked as though he might throttle Claudius on the doorstep. Thecla glanced at her husband, squeezed his arm.

"Trajan," she said quietly. "Be calm. Later. We'll sort it out later."

Trajan struggled to master his anger. He took a deep breath.

Plainly Marietta was nervous. Claudius looked better now, though his hair still possessed the single white streak, the damage from the terrible magic he had wrought, wringing the *ka* from the cat. Claudius stepped forwards, and bowed.

"May I present my wife," he said. "Marietta Emily Verga. We were married this afternoon at the parish church of St Michael and All Angels at Middleton Marsh."

Marietta gave an anxious curtsey, clinging to the arm of her new husband. Mercy glanced at her parents. Marietta's father reddened, and he stepped forward. Trajan reached out to him.

"Wait, Frederick," he said, in a low voice. "It is too late to act now. Let the party continue. We'll discuss the situation tomorrow. Do we want to air our most private family business in company?"

Thecla looked at her husband and nodded. She turned to Frederick. He pressed his lips in a thin line. He flushed to the roots of his reddish hair and rubbed his big hands together.

"Be calm," Trajan advised, his hand still at the man's elbow. "Come and have a drink with me. We'll discuss this matter together."

Mercy could see her father was still tight with anger. Thecla stood beside him, now staring at the young bride. Frederick nodded curtly and withdrew with Trajan. Thecla tried to rekindle the party atmosphere.

"The bride and groom will dance," she said, too brightly. "Come. The musicians must strike up a wedding march."

Claudius took Marietta's hand and the crowd parted before them. He guided her through the dining room to the chamber orchestra, and put his arm about her waist. The couple began to dance, eye to eye, their faces bright with smiles. The guests applauded. Even Thecla relented a little. She handed Marietta a bunch of keys, telling her to choose a gift from the Verga family jewels. Mercy noted the keys, the same ones Marietta had shown her in the icy pond, a guide to Thecla's stash of letters, the first clue about the story of the Vergas.

The party proceeded deep into the night. The musicians played until the early hours and the feast was ravaged. Little Mercy and Chloe thundered down to greet Claudius and Marietta, delighted by news of the marriage. The servants laid the table anew, with hot chocolate laced with wine, seedcakes, plum pudding, grapes and apricots, jugs of cream. Thecla cut a cake patterned with gold leaf.

Mercy kept close to the joyful couple. Her own response to their dewy happiness was tempered by the knowledge of the angel doll in the laboratory, the ritual with the circle and the arcane pattern of words. Had Claudius already told his love about his unnatural span of years, and his plans for her eternal youth?

The guests were tiring now, sitting to sip chocolate and coffee. The musicians had retired. Little Mercy and Chloe slipped off to lie together on Mercy's bed, still whispering sleepy secrets to one another. Claudius and Marietta wandered from the party, with Mercy dogging their steps, miserable with her fearful premonition.

Claudius picked up a silver candelabra, with three candles burning. The couple laughed, leaning against each other, stopping from time to time to kiss. Marietta was a little drunk. Her breath smelled of wine and cinnamon. She burst into giggles. They meandered through the house, through the corridors, passageways, landings and stairways, to his locked laboratory.

Claudius took the key from his pocket. He hesitated outside the door. His face was serious now. Did he see Mercy? He gave no sign of it. He was caught up in the depths of the story, eager for Mercy to see for herself what would happen.

"What is it?" Marietta asked. "Do you have a surprise for me?"

Claudius nodded uneasily. "I have something important to tell you."

"What is it? Bad news? Why are you looking at me like that?"

"Don't worry," Claudius said. "Come in."

He put the candelabra on the table.

Mercy followed. The long room was tidy now, the table bare except for the glass apparatus set up in readiness. The chemical circle was freshly inscribed on the floor. A cat miaowed beyond the second door, scratching at the wood.

"Your work," Marietta said. "You've told me about it."

"Sit, Marietta," he said, drawing up two wooden chairs.

He took a deep breath. "You understand the family – my family – comes from Italy. That we have our own ways and customs."

"Yes, indeed. Which is why your brother disapproved of our marriage."

"The Verga family is a large one, with many roots and branches. A veritable tribe. We have settled in the four corners of the world, though we come from Italy, and hold it to be our home. Brothers and sisters, cousins, aunts, great uncles, parents – we have two characteristics that set us apart from other people. Firstly, some of us have rare gifts. Extraordinary powers of mind."

Marietta nodded. "I understand," she said. "The unenlightened rabble might mistake these gifts for something more sinister. For witchcraft."

Claudius nodded. "There is something more, Marietta." He swallowed, reached for her hands, and stared into her eyes.

"The family – we live to an extraordinary age."

Marietta paused for a moment. Then she laughed, with relief. "So do we," she said. "My great-grandmother survived to be ninety, and my grandmother, who is ninety-three, lives still."

"Marietta," he interrupted. "I have lived for over five hundred years, and fully expect to live for hundreds more. In fact, I am not aware of any member of the Verga family having died of old age. Through accident, or misadventure, yes. We do not grow old in the same way as ordinary people, Marietta. Grief and loss can age us, but happiness brings youth again. We are immortal. You will grow old, and I'll remain as I am. You will fade and die, while I retain my strength during the lives of our great-great-grandchildren, and beyond. We have perhaps fifty or sixty years together. A sneeze. A nothing. In all the long centuries of my life I have never loved before, and I don't want you snatched from me, like a dry leaf dropping after one short summer."

Claudius looked away from Marietta, his eyes bright with tears. Marietta just stared. Most likely, she could not credit what he had said. The words of a madman, surely?

"You're teasing me," she said. Her voice was low and sad. "It's against the laws of God for any man to live such a span. It isn't possible. Tell me it's a jest. How can you tell me you are immune to the years when I see this?"

170

She stretched out her hand, where the wedding ring shone, and touched the flash of white in his hair. Claudius jumped to his feet, and strode up and down the room in a state of agitation. Marietta began to weep. Did she believe him? Did she think she had married a lunatic? His conviction was absolute.

Claudius rubbed his face in his hands. He unlocked the second door and a cat sprang out. White and tabby, the cat rushed to Claudius and rubbed against his legs, purring. Had Claudius returned the *ka* to the flesh and blood body of the cat? Mercy stared, as the creature arched its back to be petted. A real cat. Not the animated horror.

No, no. Look closely. It was the artifice. Yes. The cloth now entirely covered the innards of wood, copper wire, horse hair and sawdust. Though the workings of the cloth cat were obscured, this did not explain the complete illusion of tabby and white reality. If she hadn't known the truth, would Mercy have even noticed the cat wasn't real? Maybe the *ka* had embedded itself now. The cat soul believed it was truly a cat, casting a glamour over the constructed body with its own cat will, its self-belief. Clearly, Marietta had not seen anything untoward. She stared at the cat in puzzlement.

Mercy was taken aback by the reality of the artificial cat. Had Claudius known how effective the transformation would become? If the same thing happened when Marietta's *ka* transferred to the doll, no one would ever know she was anything other than ordinary flesh and blood.

"You see my cat?" Claudius said. "Isn't she lovely?" He stooped to pick her up. The cat pressed her face into the palm of his hand.

Marietta nodded, uncertain where the conversation was leading.

"Stroke her," he said. "Feel how soft she is, how warm. Do you notice anything unusual about her?"

"Nothing," Marietta said. "Next you will tell me she is also a Verga, and maybe has lived a thousand years."

"She was born four months ago," he said. "You are partly right – she will live for ever. If I mend her body she will endure past the ages of this house, when her brothers and sisters are dust. She will live for so long because that is a gift I have granted her. And I can give it to you too, Marietta."

Marietta gave a frightened laugh. Her hands were shaking.

"Look." He tucked his fingers under the cat's chin and made a small rip in the fabric of the creature's hide. Marietta recoiled. He pushed the cat towards her, pulling up its head, to expose fabric, stitching, the piece of parchment trapping the *ka* inside the artificial body.

"You see?" he said. "I built a body for the cat, to house its eternal soul. When mortal flesh wears out, the body dies and the soul flies away. When elements of the cat's body break or degenerate, I can simply replace them."

Claudius replaced the fabric in the creature's throat, and set it on the floor, where it sat and began to lick its tail, to all intents and purposes, an ordinary cat. Marietta stared,

172

without a word, in a blank state of shock. Mercy longed to reach out, to take her away from Claudius, from the chilly room. Claudius ploughed on.

"Come," he said, reaching for her hand. "See what I've made for you." He picked up the candelabra and led her to the second room. He urged her to kneel beside him, by the long wooden chest. Mercy beheld the newlyweds, side by side, in a curious parody of the wedding ceremony they had so recently celebrated. Claudius lifted the lid and drew back the veil of silk. He raised the candles, to throw the flickering light on the contents of the box. Marietta gasped.

The doll had lost none of its unearthly beauty. Like a sleeping princess she lay in her bed, lips parted, waiting for the prince's kiss to bring her back to life. In the warm, uneven light you could fancy she drew breath. Her angel skin glimmered. Did a faint blush steal across her cheek? Marietta stared and stared.

"Is that how you see me?" she asked. "Am I as beautiful as that?"

"More beautiful," Claudius said. "And you will live for ever."

"You wish to take the soul from my body, and lodge it inside this?" she said, in wonderment.

"Yes!" said Claudius, enthused. "Yes. Tonight! Everything is ready."

"And if I don't, I will age and die, while you remain young and hale." She sat back on her heels, the white and silver dress

173

pooling around her. Her eyes were fixed on the doll's face. Claudius continued to talk, explaining how they would live, the places he would show her. The mountains of Greece, the desert cities of Rajasthan, the blossoming orange groves in the old country.

The words washed over Marietta. She continued to gaze at the doll, tears trickling down her cheeks, an endless stream. Was Claudius oblivious to her grief? He turned away, busying himself with the tools of the transformation.

Marietta rose to her feet and stumbled from the room. Away from the candelabra she struggled in darkness, from the laboratory and out, along the pitchy corridors of Century's winter night. Claudius was caught up in his preparations and didn't notice she had gone. Then he turned to speak, flustered, and called her name. He hurried after her.

"Marietta!" he called. "Marietta, come back. I know you're afraid."

He hurried after, listening for the sound of her shoes in the empty passageways. He lifted the candelabra, in a flare of yellow light, to east and west. He slammed the door and set off in search.

"Marietta, don't leave me," he shouted. "Marietta! Come back! Talk to me."

He ran off. The house fell silent.

Gifted with hindsight, Mercy knew precisely where to find Marietta. Events in the past could not be altered. Mercy could only observe. She didn't hurry.

Distillery Meadow, the pond a black pocket in the corner. The ice was thin. To the east, the sun sent its first rays over the eastern horizon. A new moon rose. While Claudius and the family searched the house, Marietta was sitting on the banks of the pond. She had a bottle of brandy, and she sipped the burning drink as she cried. A rook flew overhead, with a hoarse greeting. Marietta thought and cried and thought again.

Mercy sat on the opposite bank, her heart aching to see the woman's pain and its inevitable ending. At last Marietta threw the empty bottle into the pond. It punched a hole through the ice and sank into the water. She gathered stones and tucked them into the hem of her great skirts. She still had Thecla's keys, and she dropped them into the pond.

The ice snapped and crackled as Marietta dropped into the pond and waded out, towards the centre. Perhaps she didn't feel the cold, heated by the brandy. The dress seemed to blacken. Pond weed caught around her arms. She stood a moment, the water reaching her chest. She took a last, anguished look at the rising sun and dropped forward into the clear, bitter water. The pond swallowed her up.

IX

Mercy stood up and slowly walked back to the house. Grey clouds massed, choking the first early sunlight, like a shroud.

Claudius ran down to the party, shouting that Marietta was missing. The house was in uproar. The guests were departing in a hurry. Claudius hunted for Marietta in a state of desperation; the servants were enlisted in searching the house. His face was white as chalk, eyes glittering and feverish. Thecla tried to comfort him, but Claudius would not be still. Soon everyone had left the house, except for Marietta's father, Frederick, and upstairs, overlooked, Chloe sleeping beside little Mercy in the bedroom. Frederick and Trajan drank and argued in the library.

The ruins of the party lay about the house. Remnants of food, soiled plates, discarded bottles and glasses. White roses dropped their petals. The bright holly leaves had lost their gloss, tainted by smoke and heat.

No one could find Marietta in the house. Claudius turned

his attention to the gardens and the stable yard. He summoned the grooms to search the arboretum, the boathouse and the environs of the lake. The first snowflakes fell, soft and plump as feathers. Soon the air was thick with snow. The gardens whitened.

Mercy wandered, disconsolate, about the house. It was only a matter of time. Somehow she had to endure this, the waiting and the hurt, in order to understand the past, and to grant herself a future. She retreated to the nursery parlour with her red book. She wrote about the party, and the demise of Marietta. Then she stood at the window and stared at the snow while the horrible events played out all around her. She wanted to help, and to reach out to Claudius and her parents. It didn't feel right, to be here, looking on while they suffered. But she didn't know what else to do. The tragedy unwound.

A shrill cry echoed around the house. Mercy tucked the book under her arm, and followed the sound to its source, in the hall. The front doors had blown open, and a gust of snow blew into the house. Claudius stood in the doorway, a dark, lifeless shape lying heavy in his arms. One of the servants had screamed – Thecla's maid, her face weary after the long, sleepless night. She stood by the door, beholding Claudius and his cold burden, both dripping water. Marietta's hair, a drowned red, hung in long, soaked strands halfway to the floor, twined with pond weed. Claudius stepped inside.

Thecla hurried to the hall.

"Oh, my Lord," she said. "Oh, my Lord. Bring her inside, Claudius. Is it too late? Is she dead? Shut the door. Quickly."

The girl woke from her trance, and pulled the doors to, cutting off the billow of wind and snow.

Mercy would never forget the face of Claudius as he walked through the hall with Marietta in his arms. Perhaps she wasn't old enough, yet, to understand how lonely it would be to live for centuries, to walk the long, long path while other people bloomed and withered along the way. But she felt an intimation of it, then. She felt the shadow of his pain. Grief and loss were carved upon his flesh. His eyes were blind with rage and pain. Without a word, he walked past Thecla and carried Marietta up the long stairway to the first floor.

A child began to scream. Thecla made a small, shocked sound, and hurried after Claudius, Mercy just behind her. Chloe stood in the corridor outside little Mercy's bedroom, in the path of Claudius. He rose before her, in his soaking clothes, while water drip-dripped from Marietta's hair and skirts. Chloe wouldn't move, and Claudius couldn't pass her in the corridor. Chloe's breath came in short, shallow gasps. She pressed her hands to her face.

"What is it? What is it?" Little Mercy ran out of her bedroom, hair in disarray from her sleep. She confronted Claudius, her beloved uncle, with the cold body of his new wife pressed against his chest. She didn't scream.

"Come away, Chloe," she said gently. "Come away. With me."

Little Mercy reached out to take the hand of her friend. But Chloe ran away, down the corridor, and little Mercy set off after her. Claudius walked on without a word.

He took Marietta into the guest bedroom with the panelling, where Mercy had found the doorway. He drew back the covers, and laid the body between clean, white sheets. He straightened Marietta's head upon the pillow, brushing back wet skeins of hair from the white face, the skin almost translucent, the lips blue and mauve with cold. Claudius leaned forward and kissed her, once. His hot tears leaked, and fell upon Marietta's face. If fifty years of marriage had seemed too short a time for him to endure, how must he feel now, to lose her after a day?

Thecla appeared at his side. "Claudius," she whispered. "Claudius, I am so sorry. How did this happen? Did she fall?"

Claudius held his wife's pale hand. "I found her in the pond at the bottom of the meadow," he said. "I told her about the family. She weighted her dress with stones."

Thecla blinked. Her hands trembled. She didn't speak for a time. Claudius rubbed the hand, a vain attempt to restore warmth.

"Of course you and Trajan were right," Claudius said bitterly. "Didn't you warn me? Didn't you beg me to break it off? I've never loved anyone as I love Marietta. There was nothing I wouldn't have done. Now it's too late."

"I'm so sorry," Thecla repeated.

The bedroom door banged open, hitting the panelled wall.

Marietta's father, Frederick, strode into the room, with Trajan close behind. The rumour had flown around the house.

"Where is she?" he shouted, pushing Claudius away from the bed. "My girl, where is she?" The words fell away. Frederick dropped to his knees and placed his hand upon Marietta's icy forehead. There was no mistake. She was utterly, irredeemably dead. The ugly, resolute man began to sob like a child, helpless and overcome. Thecla tried to comfort him, but her words didn't make the slightest impression. Finally Trajan persuaded Frederick to come away from the bedside, to find him a place of privacy, to offer another drink.

Claudius looked blank now, emotion washed out of him. He took up his seat by the side of the bed. Outside, the snow whirled and the wind moaned around the chimneys. Thecla urged Claudius to change his sodden clothes, but he refused to move. Thecla retired to her own room and changed her dress and the red jewels for a plain black gown. Mercy followed her.

"It's the end of us." Trajan entered the room and sat upon the edge of their carved bed. He rubbed his face with his hands.

"We shall have to move again," he said, head bowed. "I am so sorry, Thecla. The poor girl. Her father's distraught. I was not careful enough. I didn't think – I didn't think Claudius would go so far. So many questions will be asked. They will want to know why she died. How can we answer? I've failed you. I've failed her."

"Of course it's not the end of us," Thecla said grimly. "We shall move on again, that's all."

For the first time she looked old and tired, with shadows under her eyes. Trajan didn't move, staring at his hands, curled on his lap. His body seemed to contract.

"Stand up," Thecla said. "See to Frederick. He's suffered the worst loss. I need you, Trajan. We can't hide yet."

But he stayed where he was, eyes fixed but unseeing.

Thecla sighed, and dispatched a servant to summon the parish priest for the last rites, and another to light a fire in the room where Marietta lay. Then she returned to Claudius, to share his lonely vigil for Marietta. Time passed, every agonising minute. The priest would arrive in an hour. Claudius stared and stared, as though to memorise every detail of her face.

Downstairs, a servant called out. A word of warning. Trajan shouted. Thecla turned. What was happening?

Heavy footsteps pounded the corridor and Frederick burst into the room, a flintlock pistol thrusting forward from his right hand. Trajan followed him, and the two men struggled together for a few moments.

"You devil!" Frederick shouted at Claudius. "What have you done to her? You devil, God damn you!"

He pushed Trajan away, raised his hand, levelled the pistol. Claudius didn't move. Almost, he seemed to offer his chest. He fixed his eyes on the man's face.

"Shoot," he said. "Yes, shoot. It would be a mercy."

Frederick hesitated, perturbed by the resignation of the

182

man so firmly in his sights. The dull grey muzzle of the pistol glinted in the firelight.

"Devil," he whispered. He squeezed the trigger.

"No!" Trajan shouted. Thecla jumped forward, to push Claudius from the path of the shot. The explosion deafened. The scent of hot metal and gunpowder filled the room.

Claudius and Thecla were slumped over the bed beside Marietta, and blood leaked over the white sheets. Trajan gave a strangled cry. He ran forward and lifted Thecla. Blood quickly soaked her dress, running into her golden hair. A thin red thread unwound from her lips.

Claudius sat up and shook his head. Frederick, aghast, realised what had happened. He regarded the gun with horror. He dropped it, still smoking, to the floor and backed out of the room.

"Go away!" Claudius shouted. "You should have killed me! You fool! Go away!" He stood up and advanced upon the stricken man.

"Go!" Claudius said. "Leave us. Never come back!"

Frederick groaned. He staggered down the stairs and out of the house. Mercy heard him call for a horse, and for his younger daughter, Chloe. Mercy ran to the window, and watched him swing up into the saddle. Chloe, in a dark cloak, was lifted by a footman and seated awkwardly in front of Frederick, while the horse stamped and wheeled in the wind. Then father and daughter galloped away, down the drive through the snow. Mercy remembered the picture in Trajan's *Century* – the horseman galloping from the house. This would be the last time Mercy ever saw her friend. She pressed her cheek against the cold glass, straining her eyes to see the horse to the very last moment, when it was swallowed up by the whiteness.

They were riding at a breakneck pace, but to no avail. Neither Frederick nor Chloe would ever escape the devastation the Verga family had wrought upon them. Numbed, Mercy turned away from the window, back to the scene unwinding in the bedroom.

Trajan was sitting on the bed, Thecla's head lay cradled upon his lap. Her breath grew shallow.

"Do you remember the house in the old country?" she whispered. "Will you love me for a thousand years?"

Trajan's face, like a skull, white with shock. "For ten thousand." His voice trembled. "For ever. Without you, life will have no meaning for me. How can I carry on?"

"I've never feared death," Thecla said. How composed she was, how calm. "It has always seemed so far away. Now I feel its breath upon my face and I'm not afraid. Do you wonder where the soul travels, when the body dies?"

"I'll follow you," he said. "You mustn't leave me here, alone."

"No," Thecla said. "No, you must look after the girls. Are they here? Let me see them."

Little Mercy and Charity had crept into the room. Now they came to her, Charity in tears, little Mercy blank-faced with horror.

184

"I love you," she told them. "I love you so much. Care for each other." She swallowed, and struggled to breathe.

"I'm thirsty," she whispered. "And I'm cold." Her voice began to fade.

Aurelia took the little girls away.

Mercy watched her mother die, Trajan bent over, stroking Thecla's face, like a child. So tender he was, brushing strands of hair from her cheek. He carried her to their bedroom, and when he had laid her upon the bed he called for a bowl of water and wiped the blood from her skin. The servants drew the curtains and shutters around the house, shutting out the light, foreshadowing the eternal darkness the house would endure. Thecla's maid was sitting in her mistress's room, sobbing. But Trajan would not allow anyone to touch Thecla, fussing over her, taking the shoes from her feet, brushing out her hair. Little Mercy and Charity huddled together in the nursery parlour, unable as yet to take in the significance of the day's events.

Mercy waited patiently in the bedroom, for a last glimpse of her mother. She wanted to reach out to Trajan, to comfort him. He looked so small and alone.

She watched him straighten Thecla's dress, and light candles at the bedside. Finally he barked an order to Thecla's maid and left the room. The maid finished tidying. She gave her mistress a long, last look, then she too left the room. Mercy was alone with her mother.

She remembered so little about Thecla. If little Mercy was

ten when Thecla died, wouldn't she still have a treasury of childhood memories? Stories and cuddles, walks and meals, excursions and laughter? These had happened, surely. In locking away the events of the past, Trajan had taken away her mother's most precious legacy. Mercy studied her mother's face, and felt her heart was breaking. It wasn't fair. She wanted her mother so much. She wanted her to be alive.

Claudius, at the beginning, had promised she would see her mother, and the promise had been kept. But Thecla had endured only a repetitive phantom life, in Trajan's spheres of the past. He had embroidered her soul in his tapestry of time. Claudius had given Mercy the chance to see her mother again and surely that was in Trajan's mind too, when he set up the enchantment to hide the house from the world. He was trying to keep hold of Thecla's life, even in its endless repeating and unchanging form. If that was the case, Trajan did not seem so much better than Claudius after all.

Where was Trajan now?

Mercy had an uneasy feeling. She took up the red book, and left her mother's room. She had to find her father.

Downstairs the servants were busy clearing the house. The atmosphere was subdued. Trajan was not to be found in the library or the hothouses, his usual haunts. It was possible he had gone outside to walk or ride, an attempt to clear his mind. Mercy stalled, not knowing what to try next, but convinced something important was about to happen. She sensed this chapter wouldn't end until . . . until what?

The locked laboratory. The angel doll, the pile of ancient books. Mercy picked up her damaged skirts and ran.

The two men were standing in the first of the joined rooms, arguing. Trajan's childlike grief had flipped into violent fury. Of course he blamed Claudius for Thecla's death. He wanted to know exactly why Marietta had drowned in the pond. Claudius was beyond anger, incapable of it. He had suffered some inner emotional collapse. He responded to the questions with single words, never contradicting his brother, agreeing everything was his own fault, that he was stupid and worthless and deserved a terrible punishment. His resignation infuriated Trajan, who wanted a rock to batter himself against, not a yielding cloud.

Perhaps Claudius understood this. He raised his hand to silence his brother and led him into the second room. He threw open the chest to reveal Marietta's second self. Lifeless, like the original. Trajan was stunned. He bent over, to study the fairy face. His hand strayed, to touch the silk cheek.

"You made this?" he said.

"I arranged for her making. It was my design." Claudius didn't look at the doll. His eyes were fixed on Trajan.

"For what purpose?"

"To be a host body for Marietta's life force, so she might live for ever." Claudius showed the cat, and briefly, the parchments and old books. He explained in a level voice how the glass from Venice was employed during the process of tranferring the *ka* from one body to another. Trajan was

187

attentive. Mercy watched alternating waves of shock, revulsion and even admiration, pass over his face.

The explanation ended. Trajan stared, white-faced.

"Frederick was right to call you a devil," he said at last. "This was a devil's plan. How could you imagine she would go along with it? The process in contrary to the natural law. To God's law. It is an abomination."

Claudius roused from his apathy. He lifted his head, with a sneer.

"Who are you to talk of the natural law?" he said. "Who are we, the Vergas, to speak of God's law? How can we belong to the natural order when all God's creatures die, and we live for ever?

"If I could have saved Thecla, when she lay dying, and granted her a new life in this artificial body, wouldn't you have wanted her saved?"

Trajan's body gave a jerk. "You could have saved her? You didn't tell me! You let her die, when we could have saved her?"

"What? Against the natural order? To be an abomination? You've changed your tune very swiftly, Trajan. Listen to yourself!"

Enraged, Trajan jumped forward and grabbed his brother by the throat. Trajan's momentum knocked Claudius backwards onto the table. The glass egg and its attendant pipes fell to the floor with a crash, in a multitude of fragments and splinters. Trajan's fingers tightened about his brother's neck. Claudius did not resist.

"I could kill you," Trajan said. "That's what you want, isn't it? Rather than endure your loneliness, you want to die. I shan't let you off so lightly. I will endure, for the sake of my daughters. And so shall you. I cannot let you loose, little brother. You're a danger now. I don't know what you might do next, seeing that you're capable of so much. I will keep you here in the house, with all your memories, for ever. Century will be your prison. And it will be mine too."

Trajan stood up, releasing Claudius. They looked at each other, man to man. Trajan turned away first. Head down, he left the room.

Claudius put his own hands to his throat, bruised by Trajan's fingers. He went to the window, to view a white world, an expanse of snow, the louring clouds, the endless fall of snowflakes. He sighed, turned away, and snapped a candle from its waxy roost on a bookshelf. He lit the candle, took it to the second room and dropped it into the chest with the angel doll. He watched for a few minutes as the flames caught hold. The white face burned quickly. The fabric blackened and peeled off to reveal the glass eyes and porcelain teeth, in the underlying structure of wood and copper mesh. The long red hair ignited. Soon the chest was ablaze, the smoke acrid with the scent of burning horsehair. Claudius recoiled from the heat.

The fire spread to the rest of the room, along the floorboards into the next. Flames ate into the books and parchments. The cloth cat fled, yowling, its fabric hide alight. Mercy, and Claudius, retreated from the room.

Mercy tried to run, and like a bad dream, her feet were too heavy to lift. Claudius passed her in the passageway, and Mercy struggled to move. The fire was spreading into the corridor. The light seemed to fade, the walls stretching up, higher and higher. She collapsed to her knees. Soon the flames would catch her. She felt no heat but the smoke made her cough.

"Mercy, let me help you." She looked up. To her surprise Trajan was standing beside her, offering his hand.

"Father," she said, coughing. "You've come for me." He was older now, the Trajan of her own time, grey-haired and weary.

"Come with me," he said. "Away from here. Leave it behind. You've seen enough. I've come to take you home. It's all over now."

His voice soothed. Mercy was glad to see him. She wanted to rest and sleep. She reached out her hand and Trajan helped her to stand. They walked before the flames, along a dark corridor she had never seen before, that stretched and telescoped away.

"It's a long way home," she said. "I'm tired now."

"Keep up. Not so far."

Not so far? Days and nights and months and years. It was a long way.

At the end of the corridor Mercy's bedroom door opened. She stepped inside, to her own dusty room, and lay down on her soft, familiar bed.

Dreams of corridors and hidden closets, grand halls and dim cellars. Rising stairways with hundreds of steps. Locked towers and attics jumbled with junk. Mercy ran through the mansions of her mind, testing doors. Everywhere, empty rooms. What was she looking for? She couldn't remember, except that she must search, and couldn't stop. She had to find her way out. Nameless demons came in pursuit. Light on her dream feet, she flew down the last, long stairway to the only remaining door. The door receded, further and further. The demons drew near.

Mercy woke with a shriek. Her heart thundered. She sucked in a breath, as though she were drowning. Gasped, and breathed again. The room was dim; the twilight at the beginning, or the end, of a day. Mercy sat up, to see her wardrobe and dressing table, the writing desk beside her bed. She had returned to her own familiar bedroom. Memories tumbled in her head, a storm of images and dreams. She struggled to make sense of it, to untangle vision from reality. Trajan had brought her here, hadn't he? From the burning house. It was hard to remember.

She got out of bed. The door wouldn't open. It was locked, from the outside. Mercy drew the long curtains, shocked to see three metal bars beyond the window. The latch was nailed shut. Appalled, she understood the room was a prison. What had happened? In a panic, she hammered on the door.

"Let me out!" she shouted. "Father! Charity! Let me out!" The house was silent. Then, after a time, she heard distant footsteps hurrying towards her. Two sets of footsteps, and voices. Mercy knocked and shouted again. A jangle of keys – the lock turned. Galatea, dressed in a dull grey gown, and Trajan himself, stepped into the room.

"What is all the fuss about?" Galatea said. She carried a tray with a bowl of thin gruel and a wooden cup of water. Trajan had aged again, a stoop to his shoulders, his hair entirely grey.

"What have you done to my room?" Mercy said. "Father, why are there bars? You can let me go now. I understand everything. I won't cause any more trouble."

Trajan smiled and patted her head. He wouldn't meet her eyes. Instead he addressed Galatea.

"Poor child," he said. "You know she lost her mother. She saw the death. It turned her mind."

Mercy listened, mind blank with horror.

"I know, sir," Galatea said. "She's a difficult girl and still suffers delusions. It's good of you to take the time to visit her. She imagines things – sees people who aren't there."

"People from the past," Trajan said. "Yes. The past was so terrible she can't let it go. Maybe one day she will come to terms with those events, and be free to take up her real life again. Until then, it's too dangerous for her to be free."

"Yes sir," Galatea said. "She escaped from her room last week, and started a fire in the east wing. Fortunately, nothing valuable was damaged but we won't be able to use the space again."

"I've arranged for compensation," Trajan said. "What were you doing allowing her to wander like that? She might've come to harm."

"Sometimes she fights, sir, and struggles and bites. Like a wildcat."

Mercy broke in. "Why are you doing this? Father, it's me! What's happening?" She seized his sleeve, tugging at his arm. "Don't leave me here! You mustn't do this!"

Trajan pulled away uneasily. "I'm sorry, Mercy. It's for your own good. When you're better, I'll take you home. You must trust to the staff to take care of you and help you heal." He turned to Galatea. "It breaks my heart to see her like this."

"How long has it been, since her mother's death?" Galatea said.

"Two years now. A long time."

"And her sister?"

"Thankfully, Charity didn't take it so badly. I sent her away to school, though she comes to me in the holidays."

"It must be a comfort, to have the other one well," Galatea said, lowering her eyes.

"Mercy has always been a fanciful child, with a remarkable facility for invention and a highly developed imagination." He looked at her again, though his eyes were veiled, not seeing properly at all.

"Yes, she likes to write. We encourage it. She scribbles and scribbles her stories. I can't make sense of it – so much nonsense. I hope it helps her sort out her thoughts."

Trajan nodded. "See she gets a new gown," he said. "This one is far too small. The sleeve is coming away. Do you take her into the fresh air?"

"Yes, sir. Every day, we walk in the grounds. I only take her after dark because the sunlight seems to set her off."

Trajan turned to go, and Mercy flung herself upon him.

"Don't leave me here!" she shouted. "Take me with you! Can't you see me any more?"

He shook her off in alarm, backing out of the room while Galatea held the door with one hand and restrained Mercy with the other. The adults exchanged a glance. Galatea shut and locked the door and Mercy was left alone again. She banged against the door and hammered with her fists till her hands were grey with bruises.

She picked up the bowl of gruel and flung it against the wall with a crash.

Mercy had long hours to think about her situation. The house was silent. No one disturbed her. Were other lunatics locked up, in neighbouring rooms?

She was frightened to think she might be mad. Had she truly spent the last two years in a state of delusion? What about the long night of Century, the unfolding story of Thecla, Trajan and Marietta? She struggled to unwind fact from fantasy. It was impossible to tell which was which. A dream of darkness and imprisonment in the house, her resentment of Galatea, Trajan's distance, the concoction of a story to explain her mother's violent death. Presumably

Aurelia, too, was a warder in the asylum, perhaps a more comforting one. These things added up so neatly to become the fantasies of a lunatic locked up in a room. How could she decide what was real?

Her red book lay under her pillow, tatty and dog-eared, the pages foxed and yellow. The cover was scratched and partly burned. Galatea had mentioned her feverish scribbling. Perhaps the writing would help.

The first sentence was clear enough: *A woman under the ice.* The next sentence didn't make sense. Or the next. She flicked through the pages – she had written so much – but the long strings of words were incomprehensible. So much gibberish. Mercy dropped the book back onto the bed in despair. No wonder Trajan hadn't taken it from her. Possession of the precious red book, evidently crammed full of nonsense, showed too well how crazy she was.

Mercy wandered around the room. The wardrobe was empty. The dressing table was bare, except for a hairbrush. A single quill and a bottle of ink rested on the writing desk.

So two years had passed since Thecla's death, according to Trajan, not a century. Perhaps two years locked in this place had seemed like a hundred years. How long would she stay here? Her mind worked quickly. She could dissemble, and pretend she was better. Then Trajan would take her away.

Time stretched. Nobody came. She seemed to adjust to the new situation surprisingly quickly. A spell was falling over her, like the hypnotised half sleep in the other Century of repeating days. She found it hard to think about escape and wondered instead about the new gown. She wished she hadn't wasted the gruel because she was hungry. Oddly, the twilight didn't alter – neither brightening to day nor fading to darkness. It would be easy to give in. Living was difficult and it hurt. It would be more simple and less painful to sleep.

No. No! Mercy shook her head. She refused to succumb. She wasn't mad. Neither was she the same little girl Trajan had enchanted so many years ago. She had come so far, and seen so much. She was stronger than he knew, and she wanted to be free. Outside the sun shone, and people had friends and parties, and listened to birds and watched the flowers grow. They fell in love and argued, and never knew what the next day might hold. Mercy paced up and down the room, rubbing her hands together. She fretted. She couldn't give up now. She couldn't. What if this was yet another ploy by Trajan to stop her undoing his spell – from finding out the truth? Yes, it was a good trick. But she wasn't going to give in to Trajan's final trap. She would find a way out of here. There had to be a clue.

One more place to look. She crawled under the bed, hooked her little finger into a hole in the floorboard, and lifted a piece of wood to reveal the space underneath. She stuck her hand in, groping, and found a bundle of papers. Her fingers trembled. Mercy slithered out from under the bed. She unfolded the paper and half a dozen pen and ink drawings fell out, onto the sheets. A picture of Claudius. Another of Trajan and Thecla. Marietta, in a white dress. Mercy herself, and Charity. Another of the house, with a rider galloping away.

Mercy almost wept with relief. She tipped back her head, offering Charity a prayer of thanks. Then she turned to the letter.

Dear Mercy –

I don't know where you are or what has happened to you. Father roams round the house like a madman, tearing his hair. Galatea hides in her room. Nobody takes any notice of me, except Aurelia. Anyway, I found the paintings in the attic where you said, and I've drawn six pictures. I hope they're what you wanted. I don't know how to get these to you, so I'll put them in your secret hiding place. Did you know I discovered it? What a good thing it is that your sister is so nosey!

Sending you lots of love, brave girl. I hope you find what you're looking for.

Charity xx

Mercy pressed the letter to her heart. Tears sprang to her eyes. Well done, Charity. So she wasn't mad! Charity's hidden letters proved the truth she knew in her heart. Mercy's adventures had not been the delusions of a lunatic, locked in a cell. It was all true.

She flicked through the pages of her red book and slipped the pictures in between. Using the tatty quill, she wrote about the party, the drowning of Marietta, Frederick's revenge, and the fire in the laboratory. Even her experience of the false asylum.

Now she had to escape. The last of the five chapters remained to be discovered. The doorway, she remembered, lay in her own room behind the dressing table. She heaved it aside, picked up the book, and pressed against the wall. Was she slipping back into a realm of delusion or stepping closer to freedom? She wished for truth, and fell forward, into empty space, wondering what daylight might bring.

X

The snow had melted away. The winter day was damp and raw. Mercy walked beside her sister from the front of the house. Two horses, with black, feathered plumes, fretted in their harness. A coffin rested in the glass-sided carriage.

It was a short journey to the Verga chapel. The family – Trajan, Claudius, Charity and Mercy – walked behind the carriage, along the track to the chapel before the trees. Aurelia and Galatea, leading the servants, followed on. The wind whipped tears from Mercy's eyes. She was dressed in a black frock, with fur mittens and a cap.

Everything had changed. She was no longer Mercy the observer. She had stepped into the shoes of her former self, ten years old, following the hearse.

Nobody spoke. The wind moaned. The fields spread away, bleached and drear. The trees loomed beyond the hunched back of the chapel. From time to time, Mercy glanced at Charity, her face wan and closed, a prayer book in her hand.

Mercy had no prayer book – the book she carried was red, embossed with gold. She held it tight.

The hearse drew up outside the chapel. The family waited as the footmen stepped forward to shoulder the coffin, with its wreath of white roses and fleshy-petalled lilies. Inside the chapel, Mercy shivered. It was so cold. The coffin, open now, rested on a bier before the altar. Icy white candles burned. The air was perfumed with old stone, the ghost of incense, the breath of lilies.

Mercy, Charity and Trajan took the first pew to the right of the aisle. Claudius took the one to the left, Aurelia and Galatea behind him, the other servants further back, depending on their rank. A priest intoned the service.

Mercy didn't hear what he said. She gazed around the chapel, studying the stained-glass windows. The large panel behind the altar depicted Christ on the cross, his body paper-white, his loincloth a blaze of red. To the right and left of the window curved the wings of marble angels. Inside the coffin Thecla lay on a lining of ivory silk. Her eyes were closed, lips slightly parted. Aurelia and the maidservant had dressed the body in a dress of the palest gold. Thecla's hair was loose about her shoulders.

Mercy hadn't eaten that morning. She couldn't swallow. Now her tummy rumbled. She longed for the service to end. It seemed so irrelevant. The droning of the priest had no connection with her mother, or Mercy's feelings of hurt and loss. Her life had stopped making sense. She felt broken up and emptied out. Eleven days had passed since Thecla's death, but Mercy's life had come to a halt. She was fixed in one place. It seemed impossible for life to continue without her mother. The sun rose and set, food was placed before her, but Mercy's thoughts could not proceed beyond the moment her mother had died. She couldn't believe what had happened. Walking around the house she anticipated the sound of Thecla's voice, the appearance of her beloved face, the gentle fragrance of her body. She kept reminding herself that Thecla was dead, but her body, her heart, did not believe this could be true. It couldn't be. In a moment she would wake up. Because this wasn't right. It wasn't how it was meant to be. A world which had always been good to her now showed its perfect indifference to her suffering. Life could be snatched away. Love, despite her appeals to God, her desperate prayers and repeated wishes, could not protect her against loss.

After the service the coffin was shut again and carried out into the little graveyard where yew trees grew. The procession continued and led her to a yawning brown hole in the ground. Thecla's coffin was lowered, slowly, into this wet, muddy mouth. The priest spoke again. Trajan scooped up a handful of damp earth and dropped it onto the coffin. Charity did the same, then Mercy. She couldn't think about the face just beneath the soil. Instead she concentrated on the dirt stuck to her mittens.

Three crows circled over the chapel, cawing. One landed on the ground, wings folded, a dignified gentleman in black.

Another crow alighted on the headstone by the yew trees. The wind ruffled its feathers.

The funeral was over. Everyone had gone.

Mercy imagined her father, trudging back to the house ahead of them. After the funeral Trajan would dismiss the servants and send them away, except for Galatea and Aurelia who had come with them from Rome. Instead he would order Aurelia to draw the curtains and close the shutters. The portraits of Thecla and Claudius had been taken down, ready to be shut away in the attic.

She pictured Trajan in the library with a red book, and writing a story about the house – a story strong enough to reshape reality. Magical words, like 'Shem' beneath the tongue of a golem. Because words define what is real, she thought, and stories are the way we make sense of everything that happens in our lives. He wrought the shape of the house with words. He described five days, granting Claudius a perfect day with Marietta, as well as one final day on the edge of the spell which Trajan would haunt like a ghost with his daughters. The scene loomed, Trajan bent over his work, concentrating on his enchantment, while the house transformed all around him, lines of past and present bent and contorted into a new shape.

So Trajan hid the past, and hypnotised them into reliving one dark day so the house could be hidden away. Outside, the world had continued on its own path, year by year.

Mercy imagined her father, one man carrying an extraordinary and unwanted power, fixing their lives in his red book. He hadn't wanted to be different. He had brought them to England to live an ordinary life. He had so rarely used his sorcerous gift. Now he used it to lock up the past and take away the future because he was afraid of the consequences of Marietta's death, and because he didn't want to live without his wife. How accurately the dark, frozen night, the endless winter where nothing every grew, reflected his own heart, frozen with grief.

Mercy, in the winter graveyard, shook her head. Thecla's grave had a marble headstone now. Clumps of snowdrops bloomed from the earth where she was buried. The wind tickled the low white heads of the flowers. Claudius had plucked one of these flowers and placed it on her pillow.

Mercy was on her own again. She stood up straight.

"Mother," she said. "I need to speak with you. I want to finish the story."

The crow upon the grass fluttered its wings, and stalked away. Otherwise the graveyard was silent.

"I think I understand what happened, but I have questions only you can answer. I know you're dead, and I think Trajan trapped a piece of you here, in the centre of his spell, so he wouldn't have to lose you altogether. Only, we're trapped too, Charity and I, and we want to live again. I need to know what to do."

The wind whipped her words away. The snowdrops nodded.

"Please," she said. "Please help me."

Mercy waited. Clouds raced. Then the air grew thick, difficult to breathe.

The ground moved. Like a coverlet, the blanket of snowdrops folded back. Beneath the web of flowers was a layer of rotted leaves, worms and hard soil. A pale hand emerged from the earth. An arm, shoulders, a face. Dirt choked her mouth and blocked her nostrils. Dragged by insects, underground creatures, the slow motion of roots, the tendrils of her hair had dispersed in a fan, which Thecla pulled loose again, carefully, and painfully.

Thecla Arcadius Verga. Buried for a century. She sat up, opened her eyes and beheld her daughter.

"Mercy," she said, with a smile. Mud smeared the pale, golden gown. "I was dreaming about your birthday party in the garden. Do you remember?"

"Yes. I do remember." Mercy's lip trembled. She looked straight into Thecla's eyes and in her memory a hundred doors burst open. Images flooded her mind from the ten years of her life before the death of her mother; times of happiness and love, burning bright, in a riot of emotions.

"I do remember," she said again, face wet with tears. "At last, I do remember. I have missed you so much. My heart has ached all the time, and I couldn't even remember your face."

Thecla held out her arms. Mercy pressed herself against her mother, face against Thecla's neck, arms wrapped around her, and she cried. How perfectly they fitted together, the curves of their bodies so gracefully embraced, and Mercy held on so tight her muscles began to ache.

Finally Mercy relented, loosening her grip.

"When you died, Trajan was so sad and afraid, he cast an enchantment over the entire house. He carved up the past into five chapters, like Russian dolls, one inside the other. And you, Mother, you are the tiniest and most important doll of all, right at the middle of his spell," she said.

"People don't see Century any more. We're locked away. We never see the sun, and we live the same day over and over. He locked Claudius up in the past as well. I think Claudius wanted to be imprisoned at first, so he could have at least one day with Marietta. Now though, even he wants to escape. You have to help me, Mother. Do you want me to break the spell? Help me write the last chapter and we'll be free, and you'll be . . . you'll be free too."

Thecla smiled again. "It does my heart such good to see you," she said. "When the enchantment is undone, my soul will be free as well – to leave the world behind. I don't know where it'll go, except the light I have to follow is a burning gold, and I so long to be there."

She wriggled on her cushion of earth and drew out a red book from the ground. The name *Century* was etched in gold upon the front. It was Trajan's sorcerous book.

"Trajan is a powerful man, even among the Vergas," she said. "He so rarely used his gift. He didn't want it. He longed to be human, like ordinary people. That's why we moved to England, to start a new life, away from the family. For all the good it did. You can't run away from yourself.

"Trajan spun an enchantment, wove a web of words to break up the past, as you've seen. He tied us up. The book tells the story of the house, and spells out its hiding away, and his inability to let me go. Write the book again. You've put the pieces together, now add the final pages. Write a new ending – a happy ending. Write how the sunshine came to Century, how the girls remembered the past and stepped out into a new world. Write that Trajan learned to live again."

Mercy nodded, holding her own copy of the book. She stood up. "I am so glad to see you again," she said. "I won't lose you again, will I? I'll remember?"

Thecla nodded. "You'll remember."

"I love you," Mercy said.

"I love you too."

The crows cawed, and flew off, high above the chapel. For a moment Mercy looked away, following their flight. When she turned again to her mother, Thecla was gone too, with the first book, melting in the wind. The blanket of snowdrops was undisturbed. The flowers shivered.

Fat with memories, Mercy hugged her own book and smiled. A sensation of warmth flowed from her poor, locked-up heart, along her arms and legs, heating the pit of her belly, her fingers and toes.

The browns and greys of winter, the scent of spring flowers, the heat of summer, autumn's fruits and fires. She would have them all. And more to come. Many, many more. She left the grave and went into the church. In the gloomy shelter of the chapel, where the sunlight dropped splinters of colour through the stained glass, Mercy wrote the happy ending. How the past shuffled like so many cards, and fell away. How darkness lifted from the great house and gardens, the parkland, meadows and lake. How Trajan, Mercy and Charity stepped out into life, looking forward to a new century and the busy world of men and women. How Thecla found peace at last, and Claudius, humbled, returned to the family in the old country.

Mercy put her pen down, and gazed at the window, the white Christ with his red sash, the tender angels with the sweep of powerful wings. She shut the book, walked down the aisle, and out of the door.

She stood in the porch, looking past the yew tree and the headstones, down the hill to the house. The world was still and poised, as though a storm brewed. Mercy could taste dust and static on the air.

The sky flickered, dark and light again. The night returned, an inverted bowl sealing over the house and grounds. Mercy felt dizzy. The blood seemed to fall away from her head, and a knot tightened in the pit of her stomach. She leaned against the stone wall, afraid she would faint. The body of the chapel itself seemed to tilt. She clutched the wall, and the book dropped from her hands and clapped against the flagstones.

Outside, the night sky began to part. Like an eggshell, the dome of darkness split from the eastern horizon, up and overhead, down again to the west. Upon either hand, the night fell away and Century stood, peeled, in the bright sunlight.

Upon the ground Mercy's red book jumped and fell open. The first page turned. Then the next, and the next, in a flutter. The text and pictures passed in a blur. Mercy pressed her back against the wall, longing for the chapel to right itself. But the spell of remaking had just begun.

Outside the wind picked up and grey clouds surged across the sky, faster and faster, streaming in a torrent. The sun hurtled through the sky, like a chariot, and sank, to rise again in the east after only a moment of darkness. The day flashed, another night, and another. The moon circled, swelling from sickle to circle, then shrinking again. The trees waxed fat with leaves, and waned to their skeletal winter shapes. Waves of acid green spread across the fields, rising and falling away. The yew tree in the graveyard grew and groaned.

Mercy, twelve again, in her ragged dress, tottered away from the wall and found her sense of balance in the accelerating years of Century's recovered past. She unbound her sooty hair and stepped out from the dancing shadows about the chapel. The ground vibrated beneath her feet. She took off her shoes, to feel the grass and the heat of the passing years. She ran down the hill, the trees extending their branches around her, twisting and straining towards the sun. Seasons of grasses and flowers rose up, blossomed and died all around her.

The surge of life caught her up, intoxicating her. She stopped under the chestnut trees, and stretched out her arms. Laughter welled up and spilled over. She couldn't help herself. She couldn't stop. She laughed as the years washed over, and the summers came in a flood, and the earth turned and was renewed. And when the laughter subsided she ran on again, caught up in the relentless tide of generation and regeneration.

The accelerated years started to slow. Century loomed before her. Mercy skirted the house, clambering up the steps into the rose garden. The windows were blank and dark. She skipped along the path, in a hurry now, wanting to see her father and sister. Where were they? The gallop of the seasons fell into a walk, and then at last, step by step, to the usual progress of days. The sun came to rest over the rooftops, at about midday on a sunny January day, with a chill breeze. The tiny spikes of bulbs thrust up through the soil. Mercy, bare of head and foot, still burned, as though her heart were a furnace, charging her limbs with heat.

She ran to the front of the house.

"Father! Charity," she shouted. "Are you there? Aurelia? Where are you?"

The front doors were shut but she heard the lock turn. The left door opened. From the dark interior of the house Charity stepped out, blinking in the sunlight.

"Mercy?" she said, shading her eyes. "Mercy, is that you? It's so bright. I can't see."

"It's me," Mercy said. Her voice was quiet. Charity looked so frail. Like an old woman in an antique child's dress. She didn't even move like a child. Mercy's heart ached to see her. Charity crept out, pulling her shawl over her shoulders, averting her face from the sun. Mercy stepped closer, holding out her hands.

209

"Did you find my drawings?" Charity said. "Did it work?"

Mercy enfolded her little sister in her arms. "Of course," she said. "Look at the sun! Can't you feel it? Our lives can start again."

"It dazzles me," Charity said. She peeped out cautiously, over Mercy's arm. "Everything's so green." She blinked, eyes watering in the sunlight as she became accustomed to the glare.

"How did you do it, clever girl?" Charity said. "How did you get the sun back?"

"Not just the sun. The past as well. You can remember her again. Our mother."

Charity stepped back, frowning. "Can I?"

She looked away from Mercy, into an interior distance her sister couldn't see. The moment stretched. Mercy waited, still clinging onto Charity's fingers. A robin landed on a bare branch and began to sing. The breeze blew up, lifting strands of Mercy's hair.

Then Charity laughed and stood up straight, old-ladyness falling away. "Yes," she said. Her eyes shone. "Yes, I do remember. Weren't we happy then? Wasn't it good?"

"It will be again. We can make it good," Mercy said. "We're free. The spring will come, and the flowers and the summer."

"Mercy? Charity?" Galatea stepped out. Her face was anxious. "Girls, what's happened? Mercy? What have you done?"

Aurelia followed, rubbing her hands on her apron. She approached the girls, looking Mercy up and down.

"You've grown," she said. "And Charity too. Why are you wearing Charity's old dress? Why are you so dirty?"

The rattle of questions slowed. Aurelia's face softened. Her eyes were a curious turquoise blue, very bright now, as though a veil had been lifted away.

"But you look so well and handsome," she said, with a quick sniff. "Even in rags. I feel like I haven't seen you properly in such a long time. What an odd day it's been." She patted Charity upon the shoulder, and reached out to push a long strand of black hair from Mercy's face. "Come inside and tidy yourselves," she said. "I'll heat lots of water. You can take a bath."

As she stepped over the threshold, Charity looked back over her shoulder at the sun upon the park.

As they moved through the body of the house, the girls ran into each of the rooms to fling open the shutters and draw the heavy curtains. The dust was spinning, as sunshine poured through the windows to alight, for the first time in a hundred years, upon furniture, paintings, rugs.

In the kitchen, Aurelia began to stoke up the fire. She sent Charity to the pump for water to fill a vast copper kettle.

"I have to find Father," Mercy said, as the housekeeper stooped to feed the fire. Aurelia stood up, wiping her hands on her apron. She looked anxious again.

"I don't know where you'll find him." She hesitated for a moment. "Be careful, Mercy."

Mercy nodded. "I won't be long," she said. "I'm very

211

hungry. When I get back – could we have something to eat? All of us together?"

She left Aurelia standing by the blazing kitchen fire. Where would Trajan be? In Thecla's room, at the bedside of the wife he had lost? In the burned-out wreck of the old servants' quarters where Trajan had fought with his brother?

Mercy was afraid to see him, and aching to see him too. Now she could remember the days she had walked with him in the budding arboretum, when he taught her the names of the trees and shrubs, and riding in the park in the autumn. How he had laughed when she made up funny stories about nymphs living in the lake.

The house seemed smaller. The labyrinth of stairways and corridors was not so complex.

Mercy's instinct led her to the library. She pushed open the door.

Trajan was sitting with his back to her, at the desk in the middle of the room. Mercy walked past him and opened the wooden shutters on the tall windows at each end. Light streamed, creating taut golden pools on the floor. Atoms of dust glittered in sunbeams, which alighted upon Trajan's stooped shoulders and bent head. Mercy stood in front of him, trying to see his face.

"Father?" she said gently. "I'm sorry I had to disobey you. But I'm not sorry for what I've done."

Trajan remained as he was.

"I'll go away if you want. I'll leave the house. I know you

212

think I've put you in danger. But I've hardly lived. There is so much for us to see and do. We were dying, locked away in the night. I want to grow up. I want to step out and meet people. I want to find out about our family."

Still Trajan made no reply, and for a moment Mercy was afraid something dreadful had happened – that his heart had stopped, or perhaps he had suffered some kind of seizure. But this was a foolish thought. The Verga family lived for ever. She stretched out her hand and touched the top of his head with the tips of her fingers.

"Father?" she said. Her voice trembled. Trajan slowly raised his face and looked into her eyes.

"Mercy," he said. His voice was thin and hoarse. He took a deep breath and coughed, as though his throat was full of dust.

"I thought – I thought you were dead!" she said.

Trajan's stiff white face warmed, with the ghost of a smile. "Don't be silly," he said. "We don't die so easily."

Mercy waited for him to speak again, trying to work out his mood. Trajan stretched out his arms and fingers, easing the muscles. He rubbed his face, just as if he had woken from a deep sleep. Upon the desk in front of him lay the remains of a book. The red cover lay open. The pages had mouldered away and fallen apart.

"You don't have to leave the house," he said, struggling to find the words. "You have bested me, Mercy. Nothing I threw in your path could stop you." He blinked, eyes watering. "You remind me of her so much," he said.

Mercy swallowed. "Don't you love me too?" she said, in a small voice.

Trajan looked at her quickly. "Mercy," he said gently. "I couldn't live without your mother. I was a coward. I couldn't face the world without her and neither could I bear the knowledge of Frederick's loss or my brother's despair. My world had fallen apart. It seemed so much easier to hide and hold on to the past."

"So – you're not angry with me?" Mercy said. Her burden of guilt began to lighten.

Trajan stood up. He smiled again. This time the smile was warm. Colour rose in his cheeks.

"No, I'm not angry," he said. "I shut up the house in a long, dark winter night. It seemed appropriate then. My heart was cold. Life seemed a wasteland where nothing could ever grow again. No hope of renewal. I wanted an endless sleep. But I was selfish, Mercy. I didn't think of you and Charity. Your need for life was stronger than my desire for the end of it."

"So – we can live again, at Century?"

"Yes," he said. "Yes, we can."

He moved away from Mercy to stand in the sunlight by the window and gaze over the park. Mercy followed him.

"How do you feel now?" Mercy asked, peering into his face. "Does it still hurt so much, losing Mother?"

Trajan looked down at her. "Of course," he said. "It comes in waves. It isn't always bad. And to make up for her loss I do have you and Charity. I've missed you both. I feel afraid, because the world outside has changed so much in a hundred years. And I'm afraid because I don't know how we shall live when we're different to everyone else. But that is a very old fear, and I am used to it. I'm keen to inspect the plants in the arboretum and the hothouses, and I feel very hungry – so I suggest we go to the kitchen and hope Aurelia can cook us an enormous meal. We have a great deal of catching up to do."

He held out his hand, and Mercy grasped it tightly.

"Come along," he said. "It's time to go."

It took Aurelia some scrubbing to remove the soot from Mercy's skin and hair. She filled a tin bath with hot water, by the fire. Charity was sitting on the other side of the kitchen table, laughing and swinging her legs. Mercy complained when the comb tugged at knots in her thick, wet hair. When Aurelia scolded, Mercy put her arms around the strong, bony body of the housekeeper and pressed her damp face hard against Aurelia's body, until Aurelia stopped scolding and began to sniff instead, wiping her eyes with the back of her hand.

Neither Charity nor Mercy had a dress that would fit so Galatea picked out clothes from their mother's wardrobe, and while these were just as frail and faded, at least the buttons met at the back. Charity folded up the sleeves. Mercy wore her pearl earrings.

They didn't see Claudius. Maybe he was already on his way from England to the old country. Mercy was secretly relieved he hadn't emerged. There were things from the past she did not want to remember too well after all.

Trajan was taken aback to see the girls in their finery. They sat together at the table in the kitchen, with Galatea and Aurelia. He had a huge bottle of wine, grey with dust, and had drunk several glasses already. Now his glass was full again. Mercy's hair shone, still loose over her shoulders. They tucked into a feast, of roast chicken and potatoes, piles of sprouts and parsnips. Everything tasted hot and good, succulent and bursting with flavour.

Afterwards, as the glowing sun began to sink, Trajan took the girls outside to watch it descend over the trees, among clouds like long, pink and gold flags.

"What shall we do tonight?" he said. "Shall we have music? Shall we read together or play cards?" His face was pink and Mercy suspected he was a little tipsy. He seemed very jolly.

"Cards," Charity said. "I can't remember how to play. You'll have to teach me again. And first you'll have to find the cards."

Trajan tipped back his head and laughed. "We'll buy some new ones," he said. "Isn't it exciting? What will the world be like out there? After a century?"

The sun disappeared, the final flames of colour dying away beneath the clouds. Trajan took the girls' hands and led them back to the house.

Afterword

Mercy and Charity were sitting in the nursery parlour with their father, who read aloud from the pages of *The Enchanter's Daughter*. Galatea was fussing over a piece of embroidery. Mercy gazed at Trajan's face, identifying the features repeated in her own, and Charity's face. As though features were never truly your own, only borrowed. Loaned, handed down, reshaped. A family treasury handed out in shares, parent to child, again and again.

Trajan stopped reading, to sip from a cup of tea. In the cover of the storybook Mercy's named was inscribed beneath her mother's. Mercy Galliena Verga. An inheritance. A cycle of generations.

"Where do you think Claudius has gone?" she asked.

"I don't know," said Trajan. "Let us suppose he's making his own way. He'll find the family in Italy."

Aurelia, looking younger now, had ordered new clothes for the girls. Fashions had changed. She filled the house with

217

flowers, and began to enlist new staff. Outside, on the lawns, mauve and golden crocuses lifted their heads.

At night they dined together, and Trajan raised his glass to toast the new family. Charity giggled and Galatea scolded.

Mercy studied them, one by one. Did Trajan truly believe in renewal? Like the snowdrops, lifting their heads in the darkest midwinter, in the ice and snow? But Mercy knew her own difference, how she was set apart. How could she escape the pattern when the matter of making up their minds and hearts was fixed? Best not to think about it too hard. Best not to contemplate the passion and loss, death and loneliness. For the food was good. The pastries were particularly fine and sweet. Candlelight played upon their faces.

Here, now. The moment swelled. Mercy's eyes blurred.

"What is the matter with Mercy?" Charity said. "She's crying."

Trajan smiled gently. "Leave your sister. Let her eat. It's hard to wake up after so long. The heart stirs."

Mercy nodded, wiping her face, and Aurelia took away the plates.

A wave of daffodils rose up, and fell away. The fruit trees in the orchard swelled with blossom. Mercy stared from her customary place at the tall window on the first floor. Stiff, waxy flowers like candles bloomed upon the horse chestnut trees, by the drive. She often walked for hours in the sunshine, reacquainting herself with the grounds. As yet, she hadn't strayed beyond the gatehouse, though carriages passed frequently along the highway. The world beckoned, but she wasn't ready for it yet.

One morning two walkers progressed along the drive. A man and a woman, Mercy saw. She watched them, as they made their way to the house. The man wore a stove-pipe hat, a surprising modern fashion.

The couple were young and a little nervous. They dithered on the stone stairs. Finally the man raised a cane with a silver head and knocked on the front doors.

They were shown into the downstairs parlour. Galatea ordered tea. Aurelia told the girls to tidy up, and led them in to meet the visitors.

"We've taken on Langley House," the young man said. "The agent didn't mention we had neighbours. I had no idea your house was here, until my wife noticed it, through the trees, a few weeks ago. Such a big place, to overlook. We thought we should introduce ourselves."

Trajan nodded to the girls. "These are my daughters, Mercy and Charity," he said. They smiled, paralysed with shyness.

"Mr and Mrs Mason have invited us to visit them," Trajan said.

"Yes!" the woman exclaimed. She was young and blonde and pretty. "You must both come to tea. Mr Verga tells me you are keen readers. I have so many novels you may borrow – as long as your father agrees."

"That would be – delightful!" Charity said. "And I love

your dress, Mrs Mason. It's beautiful. Look, Mercy. All printed with rosebuds. And your hair – you've arranged it so prettily. Will you show me how to do mine?"

Charity rattled on. Trajan interrupted.

"You must forgive my daughter's enthusiasm," he said. "I'm a widower. The girls lack the influence of a mother."

The couple made sympathetic noises. Mrs Mason repeated her invitation and a date was set.

Mercy was alarmed and thrilled in equal measures. Later, she gazed at the twilight from the front window. She had recovered the red book from the chapel. Now it was time to write the last, last words.

Which were these.

The light fades. The trees are still now. The world is a remarkable, beautiful place.